Praise for the Black Knight Chronicles

"This is another great book in what will hopefully be a large and successful series. I know I will be eagerly awaiting the next installment."
—*Indie Book Blog*

In the second volume of The Black Knight Chronicles (the non-sparkly vampire series with serious snark), vampire detectives Jimmy Black and Greg Knightwood investigate a series of assaults plaguing the alleys of Charlotte, North Carolina. The string of hate crimes becomes personal when Jimmy's just-maybe-main-squeeze Detective Sabrina Law's cousin is attacked. Helping a lady out could get the boys killed when they end up in Faerie. Before long they're up to their butts in trolls, dark fae and a grand battle royal. The odds are against them, but to the boys, this is just another day on the night shift. If the night shift included a steel cage match of supernaturals.

Back in Black

Black Knight Chronicles, Vol. 2

by

John G. Hartness

Bell Bridge Books

Bell Bridge Books
PO BOX 300921
Memphis, TN 38130
Print ISBN: 978-1-61194-175-3

Bell Bridge Books is an Imprint of BelleBooks, Inc.

A trade paperback edition of this book was published by Falstaff Books in 2010.

We at BelleBooks enjoy hearing from readers.
Visit our websites – www.BelleBooks.com and www.BellBridgeBooks.com.

10 9 8 7 6 5 4 3 2 1

Cover design: Debra Dixon
Interior design: Hank Smith
Photo credits:
Cover art © Christine Griffin

:Lbb:01:

Chapter 1

A vampire and a cop walk into a bar . . .

I so wish that was a joke instead of my agenda for the evening, but we really were pulling into a bar parking lot. There were a lot of Harleys lined up out front of the club, and while that's usually a good sign for me, this wasn't my usual hangout. My comfort level was already low—this visit wasn't my idea, and my escort for the evening was Detective Sabrina Law, the exceptionally attractive investigator for the Charlotte-Mecklenburg Police Department who had helped me save the world from plunging into Hell a couple of months ago. And, until today, I hadn't heard from her after our bout of hero-for-hire. Not so much as a peep for eight weeks and four days, not that I was counting.

I looked around the parking lot, taking note of the still-running limo parked at the front door and the *click-click-click* of the cooling Harley engines parked behind it, and pulled my coat tight around me against the January chill. I didn't feel the cold—vampires don't feel cold, but nerves about whatever mess Sabrina had gotten me into were giving me a chill or two. I took a deep breath, held out my arm for my "date," and started across the asphalt toward our oh-so-sleazy destination.

The strip club formerly known as Heaven on Earth had been renamed Fallen Angel's when the last proprietor got his express ticket back to heaven punched. The apostrophe was in the correct place on the sign, but nobody knew that outside a select few supernatural types. Phil, the last owner, had really been a fallen angel, and Lilith, the immortal whatever-she-was who took over Phil's business operations when he left, had a wicked sense of humor. And a wicked sense of everything else.

When Phil had been around, the club had been pretty upscale as strip clubs went. A strict dress code had meant that Greg Knight, my partner in Black Knight Investigations, and I'd had to do laundry whenever we were on surveillance there. Under the previous management there had been more luxury cars in the parking lot than pickup trucks, and the girls had looked like they'd stepped off the pages of *Playboy*. Phil's attention to detail had helped set the tone, garnered the "classy" strip club customers.

More than the name changed when Phil left the place in Lilith's unwilling hands. Apparently the original "other woman" had lost a bet to Phil, chaining her to his business interests for five hundred years. I was around when Lilith figured that out, and she hadn't been happy. So she had surrounded herself with people more to her liking, which meant that Fallen Angel's catered to a slightly different clientele than it had when it was Heaven on Earth.

I looked at the bar and then the woman who'd be going inside with me. *One of these things is not like the other.* Detective Sabrina Law was going to stick out like a banana in a smokehouse, a fact that I tried to impress upon her when she showed up in my bedroom, yanking me from a particularly pleasant and very specific dream featuring her, a case of whipped cream, and three Daleks. Don't ask.

She shook me awake and waved her badge in my face, leaving me no doubt that I'd been talking in my sleep again, and that she'd heard me. She wasn't smiling when she looked down at me and said, "I need to see Lilith. You're going with."

I wasn't really any happier, because my best friend, roommate, fellow vampire and business partner chose that exact moment to barge in without so much as a knock on my suddenly revolving bedroom door.

Greg wore kneepads, a gas mask and an apron that said "Bite the Chef" with little cartoon fangs on a yellow smiley face. He topped off the outfit with elbow-length welder's gloves and thick rubber boots. Greg looked at me, then at Sabrina, held his toilet brush high above his head and announced in a muffled voice, "Bathroom's clean! We got a case! Be ready in a jiff!" Then he turned and waddled off into his bedroom to change out of his haz-mat gear and into his crime-fighting costume. An actual crime-fighting costume.

I watched my portly partner not close the door behind him and looked up at Sabrina. "Since you're obviously not here for a social call, you wanna wait for me in the den? There's beer in the fridge." I grabbed the corner of my sheet and started to sit up to get dressed.

Sabrina's eyes widened, and she turned to the door. "I'll be waiting. Don't screw around, this one's important."

Like the last one wasn't? Like a case where we saved Charlotte from becoming a literal Hell on Earth, wasn't important? I threw on a pair of jeans and a faded X-Men T-shirt, and a few minutes later we were rolling to Fallen Angel's.

Greg and I looked over the crime scene photos on the way to the club, and we agreed with Sabrina's instincts—it looked like there was a supernatural baddy running around Charlotte, and the best place to start looking was with Lilith. I kept trying to talk Sabrina out of coming inside as we pulled into the parking lot, but for a human, she was really, really obstinate.

I was crammed into the backseat of Greg's Pontiac GTO and really looking forward to getting out of the car. "Please don't stare at anyone, or anything. Just keep your eyes on the floor, or on the girls. That's usually safe. This isn't like the clubs you're used to visiting."

"I don't frequent many strip clubs, Jimmy, but I think I can handle myself," she said.

"No, you probably can't. Leave the badge and the guns here. Greg will keep the car running in case we need to make a quick getaway. The back door is to the left-hand side of the stage. It opens right out onto Morehead Street. If things get ugly, we hit the back door running. We'll cross the bridge on Morehead and meet Greg in the Time Warner building parking lot. You good with that, partner?"

Greg nodded. "Got it. I don't like that place."

"I don't either, but we gotta talk to Lilith," I replied. "If everything goes well, we should be out in fifteen minutes."

"And if it doesn't go well?" Greg asked.

"Keep the car running."

Greg shifted into neutral, and Sabrina and I got out of the car. She put her Smith & Wesson .40 service weapon in the glove box, along with a revolver she wore strapped to one ankle. I tossed my Glock 17 into the backseat, then followed it with a Ruger LCP in an ankle holster of my own. I reached under my jacket and stripped off a belt with two daggers in it, then unfastened the Velcro sheaths from my forearms and tossed those knives into the backseat as well.

I turned to see Sabrina staring at me. "What?"

"Nothing." She shook her head and turned to go into the club. We walked across the parking lot, and I watched Greg pull out onto the street. He turned right at the corner and drove a couple of blocks to the cable company parking lot. It was about a quarter-mile sprint from the back door of Fallen Angel's to the car, and I really hoped we wouldn't have to test my legs.

A pair of behemoths that looked like former NFL linebackers flanked the entrance, and one opened the door for Sabrina as we approached. "Serious bouncers," she whispered.

"Those weren't the bouncers," I said. "Those were just the doormen. The bouncers are inside."

We walked down a narrow hallway that was only dark if you were human. I could see the video cameras following our every move, and the two-way mirror along one wall. The hallway opened into a largish reception area with a dark wood desk in the center of the room. A small human woman sat behind it at a computer, a pretty blonde with not quite enough makeup to hide the bruise on her cheek.

Sabrina stiffened at the sight of the girl, and I put a hand on her elbow. I moved past Sabrina and put two twenties on the desk. "James Black and guest. I believe I'm on the approved list."

The girl smiled at me and tapped on the keyboard. "You are, sir. Enjoy your evening."

"Thank you." I stepped past the desk and a huge creature came forward from its hiding spot in the shadows of the room. It was about seven feet tall, looked to weigh about three hundred pounds of solid, blue-skinned muscle and had curling ram horns on top of its nominally human-looking face.

"Spread 'em," the ogre growled.

I held my arms outstretched obligingly, and it patted me down professionally. If the TSA hired ogres to do security, not only would they find anything people tried to smuggle onboard, nobody would ever complain. To their faces, anyway.

Sabrina stepped up and looked at the ogre. "Do you have any female security guards? I'd feel more comfortable with a woman patting me down. You understand, don't you?"

I stared at the floor, giving it everything I had to keep from laughing. The ogre looked down at the smiling detective and growled, "I am female. Now spread 'em."

I failed miserably at holding myself together and cracked up at the expression on Sabrina's face. She gave me a look that would have killed a living man and submitted to the frisking. A few more seconds, and we walked into the main body of the club.

Lilith had spared no expense in redecorating the club into some kind of strange blend between a biker bar and an H.R. Giger painting. The comfy leather couches were still along the walls, and there were several girls in various stages of undress writhing on men in something resembling time to the thumping bassline that pounded through the building. But the nice cabaret tables and chairs scattered throughout the room were gone, replaced by what looked like vintage Waffle House furnishings.

The clientele had taken a marked shift in focus as well. The bankers in suits and businessmen entertaining out-of-town clients were gone, replaced with biker types and burned-out rock n' roll roadies. But the part that had Sabrina's head on a swivel was the collection of monsters on display. There were ogres, a couple of weres of various species, a lizard-thing that I didn't know *what* the hell it was, and half a dozen variations of human magic-users, including a skinny dude sitting in a corner with a leather duster and a glowing staff. I gave him a long look, then turned away before I offended him. He could pull off the leather duster look. I never managed.

Another ogre stood just inside the door, the universal plain black T-shirt of bouncers everywhere stretched across the enormous azure landscape of his chest. He handed me a small sheet of paper.

"House rules," he grumbled.

I looked at the paper. That's exactly what was printed across the top of the page—House Rules. I read through them quickly, just to see if there was something about interrogating the other patrons on there, but they were basic strip club rules. Don't touch the dancers, pay for the dances or have your arms broken, blood rituals limited to the Champagne Room, no dark magic in public areas—the kind of thing you see everywhere. I folded it up and put it in my back pocket.

"Bad idea," the ogre grumbled.

I looked up at him, not understanding.

"Paper's magic. Burns up if you take it out of here. Burn your ass off. Might hurt."

I nodded and pulled the paper out of my pocket.

I handed it to him. "Why not give this to the next guy, then?"

He nodded and put the sheet back in the stack he was holding.

I led Sabrina to the bar that ran along the far wall of the club. The bar was the least populated section of the place, unless you count the strippers taking a break and the token crazy old dude that sits at the end of every strip club bar in America.

There was a brass rail following the curve of the bar up on the ceiling, and a slightly overweight girl was walking around the bar, shaking her shimmy in the zip code of the beat and trying to walk in her ridiculous heels. I did give her credit for her shoes, which spent a lot of time at eye level. I'd never seen stripper shoes with actual fish in them before, but she had a little tiny goldfish swimming around in each heel.

She wore a frilly little miniskirt and a lacy white thong, and one garter full of dollar bills.

I motioned for her to come over, and when she knelt in front of me, I slowly slid a five into her garter. She leaned in to give me a kiss, and I shook my head. I leaned up and whispered in her ear, "There's five bucks. Now go away. I want to drink."

Her eyes went wide, then narrowed to slits, and she stood up and flounced over to the crazy old guy and started giving him all her best moves. There were two of them—moves, that is. There was a shimmy, and there was a bounce. Neither of them were terribly impressive, but I'd done my job. She was out of the way.

The music was thankfully a little lower at the bar, so I could almost hear myself think as I leaned across the damp wood surface and ordered two Miller Lites. The bartender was ridiculously hot, as was often the case in clubs of this nature. The women you most want to see naked are not the women who take their clothes off for money. This woman was about five-three, maybe a hundred twenty pounds, with dark brown hair streaked with pink and purple falling straight halfway down her back. Her shredded Metallica T-shirt was cut low enough in the cleavage and high enough around the waist that I wondered if the cuts would meet in the middle and give me a better look at the black bra playing peekaboo with the night air.

I slid the bartender a twenty and she gave me back eight bucks and two beers. I slid that over to her and said, "We need to see Lilith."

"Not for eight bucks."

"The eight bucks was just to get your attention."

"My attention costs more than eight bucks, too." She turned away and took drink orders from a couple of guys at the other end of the bar. Sabrina elbowed me and pointed to a skinny redheaded guy at the end of the bar. The bartender said something to him too quiet for even me to hear, and he vanished down a hallway. A few minutes later she came back to me and gave me and Sabrina a long look.

"What's with the cop?"

"She's with me. We need to see Lilith."

"Lil's not here."

"Bullshit. If she wasn't here you wouldn't have sent a message back to her with the skinny ginger. You would have played dumb and tried to get more money out of me. But she told you to send us back without telling you who we are, and that drives you nuts, because you're used to knowing what's going on, but Lilith doesn't trust her underlings with shit. Now, you want to keep playing games, or do you want to get your head out of your ass and maybe save your job in the process?"

The bartender turned about eight shades of pale, then flushed deep crimson. "I hate vampires. You bastards can hear a fly fart a mile away."

"You don't have to be a vampire, or a detective, to see you sent Ginger back to the back, sweetie," Sabrina said. "Now why don't you go get Lilith like a good girl, and you and I won't have to have a conversation about the vial of coke in your bra."

I followed Sabrina's gaze and noticed a little lump in the bartender's cleavage that I'd completely overlooked before. I was paying attention to other things. Like her eyes.

"Lil will kick my ass if I take strangers back there—"

I cut her off. "I know Lilith. And I've got a pretty good idea what she'll do to you if she ever heard you call her Lil. So be a good girl, get me another beer, on the house, and tell me which one of those dickweeds over there is going to take us back to Lilith."

She reached into the cooler and handed me a brown bottle of beery goodness, then pointed to the little ginger guy.

I walked over to him, Sabrina in tow, and said, "Let's go see the boss lady."

He turned and led us through the Champagne Room, where several dancers were gyrating in g-strings on humans, ogres, a werewolf in half wolf form and a couple of creatures that I didn't recognize. I followed the official etiquette of strip clubs and didn't look too closely at another dude's lap dance. I kept my eyes on our guide, who I quickly realized had hooves instead of feet, and a lot of hair poking out of the legs of his jeans.

"Are you a faun?" I asked when we got through the VIP lounge and he opened an unmarked door to the office area.

He spun around and looked up at me, his face flashing red. "*I* am a satyr. These are deer hooves, you city-bred moron, not goat hooves. And I am not some cuddly little Narnian shithead to be swayed from my queen by an apple-cheeked human girl. Satyrs are loyal."

I made a quick mental note to find out if Narnia was real. If it was, Greg would be thumping around in every closet in North Carolina for the next hundred years. "Yeah, from what I hear satyrs are loyal to whoever can get them laid the most."

"Sounds like human loyalty, then. Come on." The satyr turned and led me down a familiar hallway.

The hall ran behind the real VIP rooms, where things the cops weren't supposed to know about went on. When Phil ran the place, he kept stuff pretty above board. I didn't expect Lilith to follow that tradition. Mr. Tumnus led us to another unmarked door and knocked.

I looked at Sabrina and said, "Please, let me handle this."

Chapter 2

Of course, her only response was to shove me and Mr. Tumnus out of the way and open the door, stepping into Lilith's office without waiting for an invitation. I shook my head and followed, hoping I'd brought enough ammo.

Lilith was sitting behind the desk facing a wall of video screens. From what I could tell, there wasn't an inch of the club except the bathroom stalls that wasn't being constantly recorded. The images flickered on and off the screens almost faster than my eye could follow. Lilith seemed to have no problem following all the action, yet another indication that she wasn't quite human. Well, that and the fact that as Adam's first wife, she was something like eleventy bajillion years old.

She stood up when we stepped through the door and turned to face us. She was dressed in a porno producer's idea of business casual, a black miniskirt that was illegal in at least seven states and three Canadian provinces, a tight white dress shirt unbuttoned to her navel over a lacy black bra that showed through with every breath, and a pair of thick black-rimmed secretary glasses. Her jet-black hair was pulled back into a tight bun with a couple of strands artfully loosened.

Lilith came around the desk and gave me a hug that was as much lap dance as anything going on in the Champagne Room, a full-body hug that oozed her lushness all over my body. I put my arms around her and patted her back awkwardly, trying to minimize contact with the woman who was molding herself to my every angle like spray insulation. When she decided she had me sufficiently off my game, she glided past me and wrapped her arms around Sabrina, burying her fingers in the detective's brown curls and pulling Sabrina's face down to hers.

Sabrina shocked me by grabbing the immortal's bun with one hand and bending her over backward. My brain shut down as she pressed her lips to Lilith's and kissed her thoroughly, wrapping her free arm around the other woman's back and pulling Lilith hard to her. They kissed for a long minute, then Sabrina straightened up, leaving Lilith panting.

Sabrina turned and walked to the bar, poured herself two fingers of scotch and took a seat in one of the chairs opposite the desk.

I collapsed into the other one, staring at her.

She gave me a little wink and looked up at Lilith. "Nice to see you again, Lilith. How've you been?"

The immortal woman straightened and glared at the ginger satyr, who was still standing in the open doorway. "Why are you here, idiot?"

He paled and backed out of the door, pulling it closed behind him.

Lilith walked slowly back to her desk chair and sat, then switched off the monitors with the press of one button and turned to face us. "Lovely to see you again, Detective Law. I'll admit, I didn't expect that level of welcome from you. But I enjoyed it." She almost purred the last bit as she leaned forward on her desk and steepled her fingers.

"Don't get used to it, Lilith. But I knew you'd play games so I thought I'd better make my moves early if I was going to stand a chance."

"And what delicious moves they were, too."

"Thanks."

"Seems to have struck our poor Mr. Black here quite dumb."

"Nah, I'm just wondering when the pillow fight starts. Or if I should be somewhere making Jell-O for you girls to wrestle in." I sipped my beer to hide my shaking hands, and I kept my legs crossed.

"How quaint. I'm sorry, James. That's not on the menu for the evening. But if there was something else you desire of me?" Lilith arched an eyebrow at me, and her hand traced her neck slowly.

I felt my hands shake a little more, and realized that Greg was right, I could never drink from her again. I'd done it twice last fall, once to keep Phil from kicking my ass, and again to fight a demon. But something in her blood was more powerful than any drug I'd ever tasted. There was an old power there, maybe a direct line to the Creator, maybe a crazy old-school sex magic. I wasn't sure which, or if it was both and something else besides, but it gave me a rush like the purest coke I'd ever tried and hooked me faster than a West Virginia high-school kid gets addicted to meth.

Yeah, in the early years I tried every drug I could get my dead hands on. Coke is awesome for vampires—it makes us even faster than we already are, and we can go days without feeding. But the crash is god-awful, and that stuff's expensive. Most addictive substances don't have an effect on us, but Lilith's blood was different. I could hear it beating in her veins, and I *wanted* it, but I knew I couldn't ever drink from her again. If I did, I'd be lost.

Sabrina cleared her throat and I snapped back to reality. She was watching me with concern.

I waved her off, then wiped the sweat off my forehead. "No thanks, Lil. I'll pass on turning into your blood-junkie tonight. We just need information, and figured since you were now providing lap dances to most of the supernatural underworld, this would be a good place to start. Loathe what you've done with the place, by the way. Really ruined a crappy thing Phil had going."

Lilith's eyes narrowed, and a line appeared between her perfectly plucked eyebrows, the only wrinkle on an otherwise flawless face. "That bastard suckered me into five centuries of servitude and then went off to play harps or some other nonsense. And he left me with a money pit of a bar that was hemorrhaging cash. Do you have any idea how hard it is to *lose* money in a strip club? It's almost impossible, but that self-righteous prick was doing it."

"I think nowadays he's a righteous prick, Lil. What with the whole un-fallen angel thing and all." I took a long sip of my beer. Her hypnotic effect on me was lessened by her shrieking like a harpy.

"Screw you, Black. I had to expand our clientele to keep the doors open. And keeping his business operations thriving was part of the bet."

"What did you bet, anyway? What do immortals wager on? The Cubs? Because even taking the ultimate long view, the Cubbies suck," I said.

"Nothing so petty. We wagered on body counts. I took Hussein, he took Pol Pot, and no matter how many sons I tried to add in to the bet, the little Cambodian still outshone my Iraqis by a good twenty percent. So now I'm Phil's bitch for the next half eon. Then he runs off back to Daddy and sticks me here." She knocked back the last of her wine and refilled the glass as Sabrina and I watched her.

Lilith sipped her wine and turned to Sabrina. "So, what was it you wanted?"

I could see Sabrina push aside the concept of wagering on thousands of deaths and try to focus on the task at hand. Finally she killed her scotch, set the glass on Lilith's desk and started. "There's been a series of beatings in the city. I believe something supernatural is behind the attacks. I want to know what you know about them."

"Well, that's direct enough. Who has been attacked?"

"Six young gay men. They were beaten and left for dead in various places around downtown. What's so funny?"

Lilith was laughing quietly, then she gestured behind her at the bank of video monitors. "Should I turn the floor show back on? I think that out of all the places in Charlotte with loud music and alcohol, this is low on the list of must-see venues for the city's gay population. Really, Detective, this is a strip club. Men, straight men, come here to watch beautiful women take their clothes off. It's the last place gay men would be caught dead. Perhaps you should try Scorpio. I understand that's more the core clientele there. Or Chasers, if you could drag your open-minded boyfriend in there." She gestured at me, and I sat up a little straighter.

"I'm open-minded," I protested.

"He's not my boyfriend," Sabrina said in exactly the same tone of voice.

"Really?" Lilith purred at us. "Are you open-minded enough to go to a gay strip club?"

"If I have to for a case, yeah. It's not high on *my* list of Friday night hot spots, but I'll do what I have to do to catch a bad guy," I said, finishing my beer.

"Well, that's where I would start."

"I wish you'd *start* by answering the question," Sabrina said.

"Whatever do you mean, Detective?" Lilith actually managed a surprised and innocent look. I guess with a billion years to practice, she took an acting class once or twice.

"I didn't ask if gay men came to your bar. I asked if you knew anything about monsters beating up people in my city. So let's try this again–what do you know about these attacks?"

"Would you believe me if I said I knew nothing?"

"Probably not." Sabrina said.

"I know nothing, Detective." Lilith leaned back and crossed one leg over another in a slow, sultry motion designed to get every male eye in the room focused on her. It worked.

"Why don't I believe you?" Sabrina asked.

"Native distrust of those more attractive than yourself?" Lilith purred.

"The day I'm worried about competition from someone who watched the signing of the Magna Carta, I'll let you know." Lilith actually flinched, just for a second, then her calm smile returned.

"Very good, Detective. You may be worth my attention after all."

"And you already have mine." Sabrina gave her a little smile of her own. I just leaned back in my chair, trying to stay out of the line of fire.

Lilith put her glass down and leaned forward, her elbows on her desk. "I assure you, Detective, I know nothing about the attacks you're investigating. You have my word."

Sabrina abruptly stood up, and I followed suit, looking from her to Lilith and back again. "Thanks, Lilith. I appreciate the help."

"You owe me one, Detective."

"I'm not going to bring you up to my friends in Vice for all the things I saw in the Champagne Room that are technically illegal in North Carolina. I think that makes us even."

"You know how it is. It's so hard to get good help nowadays. Pan will show you out." She pressed a button under the edge of her desk and turned back to the monitors. She grabbed a remote that would send Greg into paroxysms of geek-joy and ignored us completely.

I took the opportunity to raid her bar for another Miller Lite, then followed the little ginger satyr back out into the main body of the club.

"Don't suppose you want to just hang for a little while and have a couple beers?" I asked Sabrina as we passed through the entrance to the Champagne Room.

She didn't even look back at me, just kept walking toward the door. I killed my beer as I walked, which is my excuse for not seeing the five-foot gargoyle when it stepped directly into my path.

"Oof!" All the breath went out of me in a rush as I almost ran over the little guy. I looked down and there was a gray face glaring up at me. He looked like he'd just flown down off the roof of a building, except there aren't any buildings in Charlotte old enough to have gargoyles. His skin was uniformly gray, with some seriously wicked-looking fangs and claws. His leathery wings stretched out six feet on either side of him, so just stepping around him wasn't an option.

"Sorry, dude. I wasn't paying attention. Totally my fault. I apologize." I tried to step to one side, hoping he'd get the hint and tuck his wings away. He didn't. In fact, he stepped to the side to get right in front of me again.

"What are you doing here, bloodsucker?" His voice sounded like rocks grinding together, and he bared a lot of fang when he talked to me. I decided I didn't like the little dude.

"I'm leaving. Or I would be if you'd get out of the way." Sabrina had stopped a few feet away and had her cell phone out. I really hoped she was calling Greg and wasn't just going to video the beating I was probably about to receive.

"Your kind aren't welcome here. We don't like you, and your Master doesn't like you coming here. Does he know you're here?"

"I don't know what you're babbling about, Rocky. I'm just trying to leave before I break anybody." I let a little menace creep into my voice as I looked down at the grumpy wall ornament.

"You threatening me?" he rumbled.

I sighed. There was no way I was getting out of this without punching something. Which was really just fine with me. That meeting with Lilith had set me a little on edge, and a good scrap seemed like it would be just what I needed. So I never bothered to answer the gargoyle. I just punched him in the nose.

His carved-out-of-stone nose. I heard something *crack* in my fist, and my knuckles split on his rocky visage. I yelled, he laughed, and a stone fist rammed into my stomach in a punch that sent me sprawling. The bouncers didn't budge as several other patrons came over to join in a rousing game of vampire piñata. When I rolled over onto my back I looked up at the gargoyle, a werewolf, what looked like a human except for the pointy ears and a lizard-man.

"This would be a really good time to learn that turning to mist trick I saw on *Buffy*," I said.

Then the kicking started. I actually didn't mind the kicking, because other than the gargoyle, they weren't doing much damage. It hurt, sure, but they were too close to get a good kick in. But after the gargoyle tagged my shins for the third time, I figured they weren't getting tired as fast as I was getting bruised, so it was time for Plan B.

My Plan B was almost exactly like my Plan A in that it involved punching things. Except in Plan B I didn't hit the rock guy in the face with my bare hand. I rolled over a couple of times, and took cover under a cabaret table. Then I came up swinging. I smashed the table into the gargoyle's face, which had a lot better effect than my first punch. He went down in a crash of wings and granite dust.

"That went better," Sabrina said from across the room. She had a were-rat in a headlock and was punching him in the snout. A couple more short jabs, and she dropped the furry bugger on his face, out cold.

I turned my attention back to my mob of supernatural chumps and saw Pointy Ears rushing at me with a knife. I picked him up over my head, threw him at the werewolf, and they collapsed in a tangle of fur and ears. I turned to the lizard dude and got slapped across the face with his tail for my troubles.

"What do you think this is, a Spider-Man movie?" I yelled. I grabbed his tail and pulled, intending to swing him around my head and throw him far, far away, but his tail came off in my hands. I stared at the lizard-man in shock, and he growled at me.

"Do you have any idea how long it takes to grow that back? Or how hard it is to balance without it?"

He came at me, and I decided it was only fair to give him his tail back. So I hit him upside the head with it. A lot. The tail was a good six feet long, and probably two feet around at the base, so when it connected with his face, he stopped cold.

"You hit me!" he said.

"Yeah. That happens in bar fights. Are you new at this?" I reared back and clocked him in the face with his tail again.

"That hurt!"

"That's kinda the point. That whole kicking me while I was down thing didn't tickle, just, you know, FYI."

"Oh. Sorry about that. I thought it was . . . I dunno, part of the show. Like a lap dance, only violent."

"No. This is a fight. A real fight. You're not on *Jackass* or anything like that."

"Oh. Well, what am I supposed to do?"

I sighed, spun him around and shoved him at Sabrina. "Please kick this guy's ass for me."

"Not a problem," she said, planting a foot solidly in the lizard-man's groin. He went down like a sack of potatoes, and I turned away, figuring Sabrina had him handled.

Good thing, since the werewolf and elf (or whatever) had disentangled themselves and were coming at me from opposite sides. They sprang at me, so I sprang straight up. It was like something out of a Saturday morning cartoon. I grabbed a rafter, they smacked into each other and immediately went at each other's throats.

I dropped lightly down to the floor and observed the mess they were making, grabbing bottles off random tables to bash each other with, knocking over chairs, interrupting commerce, the whole nine yards. A couple of ogres were finally moving in their direction when I turned back toward the exit.

And ran straight into a fist of stone. The gargoyle had struggled to his feet and nailed me with an uppercut that almost took my head off. I flew backward a good ten feet to land flat on my back on the stage. A leggy blonde with a huge dragon tattoo on her back was spinning around the pole as I slid underneath her, completely across the stage to land on my hands and knees. I needed about half a second to get my breath back.

Then the gargoyle landed with both feet right on my shoulder blades and drove me into the cheap carpet by the stage. I learned a couple of life lessons in those few seconds. First—gargoyles are really heavy for their size. Must have something to do with being made of rock. Second—strip clubs don't vacuum the floor by the stage nearly as often as you really want them to. I felt every one of my upper ribs crack under the gargoyle's feet, and I screamed like a girl. Fortunately for my manly reputation, I couldn't be heard over the screaming of the actual girls.

The gargoyle hopped off my back, and I rolled over. I looked up at his grinning granite face and found myself laughing.

It had just been that kind of night. I thought I'd be able to help Sabrina with something simple, spend a little time with her and maybe get a kiss out of the deal. Instead I ended up flat on my back with a bunch of broken ribs in the middle of a destroyed strip club with a gargoyle ready to stomp my face flat.

"What are you laughing at, asshole?" He reached down and dragged me to my feet. "Well, at least you'll die happy." He pulled back his fist for one more massive punch, and then his ear disappeared. He dropped me and clapped one hand to the side of his head, then turned to look for the new attacker.

My partner, Greg Knightwood III, stood six feet away holding his favorite pistol, a Beretta Px4 Storm with stainless steel slide. The gun glinted in the flashing lights of the club as he leveled it at the gargoyle's head. "Wanna see what else I can shoot off?"

"My ear! You wrecked my ear! You asshole!"

"You wrecked my partner. I think we're even," Greg said.

An ogre came up behind him and started to reach for the gun. Sabrina, newly rearmed by my partner, pressed her Smith & Wesson to his ear and smiled.

"Now, now. We're leaving. But you lay a hand on my friend, and there will be some new stains on this carpet." She smiled as she said it, and I think that was the part that really worried the ogre. It sure scared the hell out of me. I shook my head and headed for the door, leaning on Greg for support. I hadn't made it three steps when Lilith appeared in front of me.

"Where the hell do you think you're going?" she demanded.

"I think I'm going home. I think I'm going to drink about six pints of blood, then about twelve beers, and then I'm going do like the myths say and sleep the whole goddamn day away because every rib is busted, I think one arm is dislocated and I'm pretty sure I broke about eleven bones in my hand punching that rock-headed son of a bitch back there. Any other questions?"

"Who's going to pay for all these damages? You wrecked my club, Black, and that doesn't come cheap."

I lost it. That's the only way I can explain going off on Lilith like I did, because most days she scares me silly. But I was in pain, a lot of pain, and my night was *not* going the way I'd hoped. I was pretty pissed about it.

"I didn't wreck your club, Lilith. Your asshole patrons wrecked your club. You know, the ones that started a fight with *me*. The fight your bouncers didn't do anything to stop. The fight you watched on your little video monitors until it was over and you could come out and make a scene. I don't know what kind of beef you guys have with vampires around here, and I sure don't know who this Master is y'all keep talking about and I don't give a shit. We're leaving. And if you want to try and stop me, we can find out just how damn immortal you are right here, right now. So, you wanna get outta my way, or you wanna dance?"

Lilith looked up at me, mouth hanging open. I guess it had been a matter of centuries since anyone had really pushed back at her, and she had forgotten how to handle it.

Then in between eyeblinks, she was pressed against me, looking up at me with eyes of fire. "Oh, we'll dance, little vampire. We shall definitely dance. But not now, and not here. You may leave. Unmolested . . . if you like. But you owe me, little vampire. And I always collect on my debts." Lilith gave me a smile that started a fire in my toes and seared me all the way to the top of my head, while simultaneously sending chills down my spine.

I motioned for Greg to help me walk, and we headed for the exit. Greg tossed Sabrina his keys, and she went on ahead of us as he half carried me out of the club.

Once we were out on the sidewalk with no one following us, I said to Greg "Thanks, pal. I don't know what I would have done without you in there."

"Probably died a horrible death. Again."

"Yeah, probably. Hey, how did you know to shoot the gargoyle's ear off to get his attention?" I asked as we walked across the bridge to where Sabrina waited with the car.

Greg didn't answer, and didn't look at me for a long moment.

I pressed. "Come on, buddy. That was really good. I mean it. I just want to know where you learned about gargoyles and how you knew that you could shoot off little parts of it even if you couldn't hurt the body."

"I didn't."

"Didn't what?"

"I didn't know all that about shooting its ears off."

"Then why did you shoot its ear off?"

"I was aiming for the back of its head. But an ogre jostled me, and I missed."

I opened my mouth to freak out on him, but Sabrina rolled up in Greg's car just then. She pulled up alongside us and opened the doors.

"Get in." She said, moving around to the passenger side. I slid into the backseat and lay down as best I could. Greg had a towel behind his seat, because he's a hoopy frood that way, so I tried to put the bloodiest parts of me on the towel to save the upholstery.

"What's up?" Greg asked Sabrina.

"I just got a call while you were in there. There's been another attack. It's just a few blocks away. Let's go."

"What's the rush?" I said as we peeled rubber out of the parking lot.

"The victim. He's my cousin."

Chapter 3

A narrow alley separated the main branch of the public library from the arts center that had once been the First Baptist Church. Now labeled Spirit Square, the old sanctuary was more likely to see an acoustic concert than a choir singing. But tonight it was blue lights instead of bluegrass music as half a dozen police cruisers and a pair of ambulances crowded into the tight space between the buildings.

Greg pulled his car into the small parking lot, and we climbed out and headed into the alley. Sabrina flashed her badge at the uniform guarding the scene, and we were in the middle of a crime scene. Again. But this time we hadn't caused any of the damage.

Sabrina hit the alley and headed straight for a tall black man in an expensive coat. He did not look happy to see us, so I waved Greg over to the side, and we stopped well out of human earshot, which of course was plenty close for us to hear every word.

We picked up the conversation a couple of sentences in, but it was clear that this guy was some kind of boss, and he totally didn't want us to be there.

"I understand your hesitation, sir, but these guys have some resources that we don't have. They have connections within the community to people who are . . . reluctant to speak with the police," Sabrina said to the tall man, who I guessed was her lieutenant.

"I appreciate that, Detective, but it's not your call to make."

"Then whose call is it, sir?" Sabrina was getting upset, and I could tell that her personal relationship with the victim was not going to do her any favors with her boss. "Either I'm the lead on this case or I'm not. And if I am the lead, then my resources are mine to do with as I see fit. If I'd rather hire a couple of investigators outside the department than just line the pockets of the same snitches all over again, I should be allowed the freedom to do that. And if I'm not . . . ."

I decided Sabrina shouldn't really give her boss that option, especially judging from the stormy look on his face, so I barged in, feigning ignorance of anything I shouldn't have been able to overhear.

"Detective Law? I was able to reschedule our other client. We'd be happy to do whatever we can for you on this case. Oh! Excuse us. Greg and I didn't realize this was a private conversation."

I extended my hand to the man, who looked at it just a second too long before shaking it with his expensive gloved one. "You must be . . . ?"

"I'm Lieutenant Joseph McDaniel. I assume you're the *private investigators* we've heard so much about."

Someday I'll meet someone over the age of twelve who doesn't say "private investigator" like it's a venereal disease, but I doubt they'll work in law enforcement.

"Well, sir, I can't vouch for what you've heard, but we're here to help any way we can." I put on my best aw-shucks face and tried not to look like I could drink every drop of blood in his oversized frame without batting an eye. Not that I thought he'd recognize that look.

"So what can we do to help, Detective?" I didn't put too much extra emphasis on "detective," but I made it pretty plain who we were here for. McDaniel's eyes flashed a little, and I could tell my subtle dig wasn't lost on him.

Sabrina led Greg and me over to one side of the alley as McDaniel made his way back to the main street where all the reporters were waiting. "Here's where it happened, at least the last of it." She indicated a wall of the library with blood smeared at least eight feet off the ground. "It looks like he was held high against the wall somehow and pummeled. The bloodstains and spatters are high."

"Maybe the guy that attacked him moonlights for the Bobcats. But those spots are high even by NBA standards," Greg wisecracked. I kicked him in the shin. "Sorry."

"How is your cousin?" I asked once the boss man was out of earshot.

"They're pretty sure he'll live, but they don't know if there's going to be brain damage. He was beaten so badly I didn't recognize him. They only knew it was Stephen when they looked in his wallet."

Just then a distraught young man ran into the alley and headed straight for the crime scene. He was well dressed, attractive and slender, with perfect hair, and tears were pouring down his face.

He got to the mouth of the alley and froze. "Sabrina?" he asked.

Sabrina turned and stared at him. "I'm sorry, sir. Do I know you?"

"I'm Alex. Alex Glindare. I'm Stephen's husband. You're his cousin Sabrina, right? I recognize you from old family pictures."

Sabrina got that deer-in-headlights look, and her head swiveled from cop to cop trying to see if anyone had heard this little tidbit.

"I gotta take care of this," I muttered to Greg.

"Take care of what?" my socially inept partner asked.

"If her supervisor knows that Sabrina has a personal relationship with one of the victims, she'll be off the case in a heartbeat. I need to quiet this guy down. You see what you can find out from the crime scene guys while I talk to him.

Everything about Alex was the picture of a modern young gay man whose partner just became a statistic. He had on a long dark wool coat over a nice suit, and his shoes probably cost more than my entire ensemble. His wardrobe screamed "bank vice president," but the tears threatening to spill down his cheeks shouted "terrified spouse."

I put an arm around his shoulders and steered him back the way he came. "I'm Jimmy, and I'm a detective. I'm here to help. So you're Stephen's partner?" I didn't bother to add the "private" to the "detective," since the longer he thought I had some official capacity, the more information he was likely to give me.

"Husband. We were married in Boston last year. Where is he?"

"He's at Presbyterian Hospital, probably still in surgery. We can get someone to take you over there as soon as you answer a few questions for us, okay?"

By now I'd gotten him to the back of an ambulance and had him sitting down on the bumper. His eyes darted around the scene, still looking for his partner while the blue and red lights painted lurid shadows down the brick alleyway. I motioned for a paramedic to bring over a cup of coffee and sat there with my arm on his shoulders until he pulled himself a little more together.

After a minute he stopped the worst of his shaking, and I asked, "Are you okay? Can I ask you a couple of questions now?" He nodded, and I went on. "What's your name?" I figured I'd start with some softballs and see how it went from there.

"Alex Glindare."

"Where were you tonight?" I knew this guy could no more cause the kind of carnage I saw in the alley than I could be a Coppertone girl, but the question had to be asked.

"I was working late. I'm in acquisitions for Wells Fargo, and you might have heard that we bought this little bank a while back." He jerked his thumb from one skyscraper to another. I knew something about banks buying each other all over town, but since I'm more of a stuff-cash-in-my-mattress kind of guy, I took him at his word.

"And where was Stephen?"

"He had rehearsal. Down the street. He was going to come meet me at the office when he was done." Alex pointed down Tryon to the Center for Dance, the new headquarters of North Carolina Dance Theatre.

"Do you know when rehearsal was due to be over?" I was trying to keep the questions simple, so he didn't have to push too hard to answer, but still felt like I was giving him some attention. Since I knew he had nothing to do with this, I could only hope that by running interference with the spouse, I was freeing Greg and Sabrina up to do the real investigating.

"He was supposed to finish up around ten, then walk down to meet me. I didn't even look up until after eleven, and when I saw what time it was, I freaked out and started calling him. His phone went straight to voice mail, so I decided to see if he was grabbing a drink at Rock Bottom or Fox & Hound. Then I saw this, and they told me a dancer had been attacked, and . . . we do this all the time, and nothing like this has ever happened."

I gave him a minute to pull himself together before starting in on the more direct questions. "Do you know anyone who would have any reason to hurt Stephen? A jilted former lover, perhaps, someone he beat out for a part in a show, anything like that?"

He took a minute to think about it before answering. I had to give him that. Most spouses in this situation sanctify the injured party, and all of a sudden a wife-beating SOB with a twelve-pack-a-day Miller habit becomes a choirboy who helps little old ladies cross the street.

"No. We've been together for more than five years now, and I'm pretty sure he's never cheated on me, and I've never cheated on him. And as far as competition at work goes, somebody might put Icy Hot in his dance belt, but I can't see a modern dancer beating someone almost to death." He gave me a wry smile. "Stereotypes exist for a reason, Detective. Gay men aren't all sissies, but we're not usually beating people up in alleys, either."

He had a point. I didn't know a whole lot about Charlotte's gay culture, but I couldn't imagine a guy putting another guy in the hospital by beating him with a ballet shoe.

"All right, Mr. Glindare, that's all we need for now. Would you like one of these officers to drive you over to the hospital, or do you think you can make it there safely on your own?"

"I'll be all right. Just, please, catch the bastard that did this to Stephen."

"We'll do everything in our power, sir." I didn't bother to mention that our power included a few things not normally in the police arsenal, but I shook his hand and headed back over to Sabrina and Greg.

Chapter 4

Sabrina and Greg were back at the blood smear with a short balding man with thick glasses who was pointing some kind of laser measuring device at the wall. Just eyeballing it, it looked like somebody had picked the victim up and slammed him against the wall a few times. Only problem with that scenario was that the bloody bricks were eight feet off the ground. So either the attacker brought a ladder to a mugging, or we were playing in the supernatural world again. Sabrina introduced me to the blood spatter expert, whose name I promptly forgot, and motioned me over to the side. Greg stayed behind to geek out over all the buttons and LEDs on the man's toys.

"What did the partner say?" she asked.

"Husband," I replied absently, going through my mental notes to prepare the recap.

"Huh?" Sabrina stopped cold and looked at me for the first time since we got to the alley. Her eyes were tinged with red, and I was pretty sure it wasn't from the wind.

"Husband. They were married out of state last year."

"Okay, what did the husband say?" Her voice was tight and there was a sharp line between her brows that I'd never seen before. I stepped closer, but she backed away, like a skittish animal.

I kept my voice low and even, trying to play it cool. "You okay?"

"No."

"You wanna talk about it?"

"Not really."

"Okay, but I'm here if you change your mind." I held out a handkerchief. "And stop drying your eyes on your scarf, you're getting mascara on it."

"You weren't supposed to notice that."

"I'm a detective, Detective." I gave her a lopsided grin. "I'm supposed to notice things."

She looked at me then, and it might have been my imagination, but I thought that line between her eyebrows might have been a little less deep than a few moments earlier. "Thanks. I appreciate it. Now, what did the partner—husband—say?"

"He doesn't know anything, nobody would want to hurt your cousin, the victim walked alone this way fairly often, blah, blah, blah."

"Kinda what I figured. There's not going to be anything here of any use, either. At least there hasn't been at any of the other scenes."

"So now what?" Not being well versed in police procedure I didn't know if we all had to stand outside for the rest of the night in freezing weather, or just her. Like I said, the cold didn't really bother me and Greg, but with no blood of our own, it took a long time to warm back up after being outside for a while.

"We go to the hospital."

"Good deal, I'm getting a little peckish." Even if my blood hookup didn't work at the hospital, they were good sources of nutrition for so many reasons.

"Oh. I guess I woke you up before breakfast, didn't I? Sorry about that. But you're not going to—"

I cut her off before she had to ask. "I've got a guy who hooks me up out of the blood bank."

"So do you go down there and buy a pint, or what?"

I wasn't sure how much I wanted to get into the details of the bloodthirst with Sabrina, but if it took her mind off her injured cousin, I'd give it a shot. "The human body holds about ten pints of blood. My body doesn't make any blood. I need to replace all ten pints at least every three days, preferably every two. And for me to be at full strength, I need ten pints daily."

"Wow. I had no idea." She looked a little pale as the red and blue flashing lights played across her face.

"Fortunately, most people don't. Now you have some idea why blood banks are always running short, even though they're constantly doing blood drives. It's not just humans and hospitals that are getting that blood. It's vampires too. And some probably aren't as thrifty as me and Greg."

"That must get expensive, and what do you do if your guy takes a vacation? Do you have to go back to . . . you know?"

"Eating on the hoof? Not always. Our guy has a nice little network of assistants and backups, and there are other places to get blood if we really need it. But sometimes, if supply gets tight, we have to hunt. Greg refuses, and he learned some kind of Zen yoga trick that lets him hibernate until the flow is restored, but I'm not against grabbing take-out from time to time."

"I guess it's just a little unnerving hearing you talk about it like that, like it's nothing." She wrapped her arms around herself a little tighter, whether from the chill or the topic I wasn't sure.

I kept my voice soft, "You guys make blood all the time. We don't. It takes you about twenty-four hours to replace a pint of lost plasma, and about a month to replace that many red blood cells. And you'll never miss it. So as long as I'm not drinking more than a pint or two at the most, the worst thing that happens is my donor feels a little woozy when they wake up. I try not to drink from anybody that looks like they're about to drive anywhere. I don't want to cause an accident. And in a few days, they're good as new. But if I don't eat, it's bad for everybody. I will get weak, then I'll get a little nuts, then I'll get really nuts, then I'll turn into a monster. Then I'll eat, with no regard for leaving anything behind, and then we've got a bigger problem."

"A new vampire."

"Yeah, a new vampire. If I go nuts and drain somebody completely, unless I take precautions, they're coming back. And most of the time, we don't want that."

"Most of the time?" She looked at me questioningly.

"Okay, I can't think of a time that I'd want to turn somebody, but it might happen. But yeah, we don't want that. So sometimes I go out for dinner. I don't go after anyone that's been fed on recently, at least as far as I can tell."

"But you guys aren't the only vampires in town, are you?"

"I'm sure we're not. There are too many of all other sorts of critters running around for us to be the only vamps, and you heard the goon in the club tonight talk about vampires and some kind of 'master.' But I don't know any others."

"And don't really want to meet any," Greg said, joining us. "Your Dr. Fishbein was very enlightening, Sabrina. As we suspected, the majority of the attack took place elsewhere, then the victim—"

"Stephen," Sabrina said in a small voice.

Greg toned down the professorial tone a bit and continued.

"Sorry, Stephen was brought here and dumped. But there was an element of the attack that took place in the alley. Apparently his head was held at nearly eight feet off the ground and beaten severely against the wall. I asked Dr. Fishbein to speculate on what could have done such a thing, but he was reluctant to do so." Greg looked a little chastened, like the blood spatter guy had spanked him over something.

"Let me guess," said Sabrina, affecting a hunched posture and nasal quality to her voice "I do not *speculate*, Mr. Knightwood. I leave that to the *detectives*."

Greg looked relieved. "Yes, exactly. I wondered what it was that he has against detectives, but I didn't want to stick my nose in where it didn't belong."

"There's a first," I said.

Sabrina snorted, and I looked over at her. It was good to see her smile again, even for a second. "He's failed his pistol qualifications seven times. It's the only thing keeping him from coming into the department and moving quickly to a gold shield, so he's a little bitter. Don't let him bother you. We've got bigger issues."

"Like what?" Greg asked as Sabrina walked past him to the car.

"We gotta go to the hospital to talk to the victim," I said, following her.

"Oh good," he exclaimed, digging for his car keys. "I'm a little hungry."

Chapter 5

Sabrina got even more withdrawn as we neared the hospital. Greg dropped us off at the front door, then went to try to find parking. Sabrina and I walked in, and the disinfectant smell of the place almost knocked me over. Hospitals weren't my favorite place when I was alive, and having enhanced senses has done nothing to endear them to me, despite the fact the place was now my main grocery store. The smell of fake lemon, ammonia and death permeates every inch of the place, and no matter what time of day or night I arrive, it's always too bright, too loud and too sterile for my taste.

I cracked a couple of lame jokes to try to lighten the mood, but nothing helped the cold shoulder I was getting. Sabrina was obviously worried about her cousin, but I felt like there was something else going on. As we walked past the nurse's station on the way to Stephen's room, I grabbed her arm and pulled her to a stop.

"What's going on?" I asked in a low voice. I didn't want a huge scene if we could avoid one, but I was not going in that room without all the information.

"What do you mean? There's nothing going on, it's just a case." She didn't look me in the eye, which is generally a good idea with vampires, but Sabrina was immune to our mojo somehow.

"Sure," I said, sarcasm dripping from my words, "It's just a case where the victim is your cousin and for some reason your heart is beating twice as fast heading to his hospital room as it was at the very bloody crime scene. So do you want to tell me what you're afraid of, or do you want to keep trying to BS a guy who can hear the very blood in your veins?"

Sabrina looked up and down the hall, and seeing no one, pulled me to a sitting area by the elevators. Greg came off the elevator just then, and I waved him over. She took a deep breath, and then said, "I wasn't telling you everything."

"Wanna move on to the things I didn't already know?" I shot back.

She took another deep breath, dashed a tear away with the back of one hand, and went on. "Stephen isn't just any cousin. He was my best friend growing up. He was like my brother."

I leaned back against the wall. "And you haven't told anybody in the department because . . ."

"Because they'd throw me off this case so fast it would make your head spin, and I'm the only detective that cares enough to actually try to find out who's doing this."

"Not to mention the only one with the appropriate extra-curricular resources to actually get anything done."

"And that."

"What else?" I asked, leaning in to make sure we weren't overheard as a nurse wheeled a cart of expensive-looking equipment past us.

"What do you mean?" Sabrina doesn't do the wide-eyed innocent look very well.

"Really? You're still going to try to lie to someone who can read your blood pressure from ten feet away?" I put a hand on her shoulder and looked in her eyes, no mojo. "Tell me. I'll do anything I can to help. And I won't even be a smart-assed jerk about it, I promise."

"Stephen wasn't exactly the golden child in our family. His parents were—are—very Southern, and very Southern Baptist." She looked from Greg to me to see if we understood what she was saying. Having grown up around here, we got it perfectly.

"So you're saying that he wasn't exactly welcome for Thanksgiving once it became obvious that he wasn't ever going to bring home any grandchildren," I said.

She put her head in her hands and talked to the floor. "Exactly. Stephen came out when we were teenagers, and it didn't go over well at school. He got beat up a lot, but it was even worse at home."

"His parents beat him for being gay?" Greg asked furiously. My partner is a real champion of the downtrodden, having gone through life as an overweight comic book nerd. Now that he's a super-strong, super-fast overweight comic book nerd, he's gotten a little self-righteous about it.

"No," Sabrina said. "They never laid a hand on him. At all. I don't think my uncle even spoke to Stevie for the last two years he lived at home. They just ignored him, pretended like they didn't have a son, and when he turned eighteen, they kicked him out."

"Just like that?" I asked.

"Yeah. He came home from a summer dance clinic to find all his belongings in boxes on the porch and the locks changed."

"That's pretty awful," I said. "But what does that have to do with you?"

"Because he called me that night. When his folks kicked him out, he called his favorite cousin Sabrina to see if he could stay with me, just until he found a place."

"So how long did he stay?" I asked.

"I didn't pick up the phone. I was still in school and needed my dad's money to cover my apartment. I knew if I helped Stevie out, my parents would cut me off. So I didn't answer. I haven't seen him since."

She still hadn't looked up, and I suspected she was afraid of what she'd see on my face.

I reached down and took her hand. "How long has it been?"

"Nine years. We were so close, it felt like I cut off my arm to abandon him like that, but I did it. And now he's lying in there hurt and I'm scared to go see him because . . ." Her words trailed off. She took a deep breath, and shoved her emotions back under control.

"Because you're afraid he'll hate you for leaving him out in the cold." I made my voice a little hard, and it had the desired effect.

Her face snapped up, and she looked at me in a sort of shock.

I went on, "He might, you know. But it's more likely he still loves you and has just been waiting for you to grow up enough to be a part of his life again. Now let's go in there and see what we can do to help him."

"How'd you get so smart all of a sudden?" Sabrina asked as she wiped her eyes and got to her feet.

"He's older than he looks, remember?" Greg chimed in. "You don't live this long without picking up a few things."

"Well, technically, you didn't live all that long." Sabrina laughed a little.

"True, but you can still learn a few things walking around dead. Now let's go have a little family reunion." I took her arm and led her down the hall to her cousin's hospital room.

Chapter 6

Stephen was unconscious, and it was probably for the best. His face looked like something that had been dragged along I-77 behind a truck for a couple of miles, and then beaten with a meat tenderizer. He had tubes coming out of every visible orifice, and three or four bags of different substances dripping into his arms. The beep-beeping of his heart monitor was steady, but I was alarmed to see the respirator pumping away. His skin had a greenish tinge to it, like nothing I'd ever seen before.

Sabrina pulled a chair over to his bedside and sat down in it, taking her cousin's hand.

"Stevie?" she asked in a small voice. I heard a little tremble, and looked up at her. The look on her face was pure murder, and I really didn't want to be the guys that hurt her cousin when she found them.

Greg and I tried very hard to be invisible while she had a moment with her cousin.

"Stevie, baby, it's Sabrina. I'm here now, little buddy. It's gonna be okay. I promise, Stevie, I'm gonna find whoever did this and I'm going to make them pay. Nobody's ever going to hurt my Stevie again, I swear to God." She put her head down on the back of his wrist.

I nodded to Greg that we should give her a minute, and we headed out into the hall.

"Did you smell that?" I asked Greg as soon as the door shut.

"Yeah, that was not the typical hospital disinfectant funk in there. It was some kind of floral smell, but something nasty under it, like decay. I've never smelled anything like it." Greg has the super-sniffer of the group.

We headed down the hall to the waiting room and almost ran face-first into a scowling Alex Glindare.

"Alex," I said when we had all recovered from our near-collision. "What's wrong? I mean, I know what's wrong, but you look pissed. Has something else happened?"

"No, I'm fine," he said in a tone that made it pretty obvious he was anything but fine. "Just a run-in with a busybody nurse. It happens."

"Oh," said Greg. "She didn't want to tell you anything because you're not family in her sense of the word?"

Sometimes my partner is really perceptive, something that's easy to overlook when he wraps himself in black spandex, which happens more often than it should.

"Exactly." Alex took a deep breath, squared his shoulders, and looked down at the floor for just a second. Once he had himself back under control, the questions poured out of him in a rush. "How is he? Is he awake? Did he tell you anything?"

"Whoa, pal. Slow down a little. He's still unconscious. Detective Law is in there with him right now, but I doubt she's learned anything else."

"Detective Law? You mean Sabrina?"

I nodded, just as Sabrina came out around the corner, her hand resting on her gun. I knew she was looking for something to shoot, and I didn't blame her. She drew up short and put on her professional mask when she saw who we were talking to.

Alex cut her off before she could say anything. "You look a lot different than in your ninth-grade yearbook, Detective."

Sabrina smiled a little before saying, "I told Stevie to burn those things. It's a pleasure to meet you, Alex."

"You, too, Cousin Sabrina. I just wish it were under better circumstances."

They stood there staring at each other for a second before I lost all control of my mouth again. "Well are you two going to hug it out so we can get on with the investigation, or would you like to just stand here in the hallway and cast meaningful glances at each other all night?"

Sabrina studiously ignored me while Alex actually laughed. He then looked around guiltily, as if someone might see him laughing and think ill of him for it.

"It's okay, Alex," I said. "You're allowed to laugh when you're supposed to cry. You're Southern, it's the way things are done down here."

He chuckled again and said, "It is indeed, isn't it? Now, what do you know about who beat the hell out of my husband?"

"Right now, nothing," Sabrina said. She made the transition into "cop mode" so quickly it made my head spin. "We found no usable forensic evidence at the scene. The alley just sees too much traffic for us to get anything definite. So now we wait to see when Stevie wakes up and we find out what he can remember. What is it?"

Alex was smiling a little, but his head snapped up at her question. "Oh, sorry. It's just that nobody calls him Stevie anymore. Nobody but me. He always said that there are only two people in the world allowed to call him Stevie. His favorite cousin and me. And here we both are."

Sabrina's eyes clouded over again, and she reached out to take his hand. "Yeah, here we are. And here we'll be until he wakes up. Then we'll go get the son of a bitch that did this and teach him what pain looks like."

"While you two are hanging out here drafting lesson plans on pain, Greg and I will start asking questions," I said.

"Who are you going to ask?" Sabrina prodded.

"We can't reveal our sources, Detective. Isn't that what you keep telling your lieutenant?" Greg replied.

"You guys usually are my sources, you dork."

"Good point, but our issues remain unchanged." My partner put on his best enigmatic smirk, which did more to make him look like he had a sour stomach than a secret, and headed down the hall.

"I have no idea what he's babbling about, but you go wait for your cousin to wake up and we'll see what we can come up with." I turned and started off toward the elevators, where a little kid was staring at Greg's utility belt.

The doors chimed open, and we all got on. The kid's mother pushed the lobby button, while Greg hit the button for the basement, where the blood bank was kept.

As they got off in the lobby, I turned to Greg and said, "Where to now, Caped Crusader?"

He flipped me off as the kid went wide-eyed out the elevator doors.

Chapter 7

The morgue wasn't nearly the creepy, poorly lit place you'd expect based on decades of popular movies and zombie video games, but my impressions of the place could be colored by the fact that I'm dead. It did have a peculiar smell to it, one that kinda lingered on my clothes after a visit. It wasn't just the stink of hospital disinfectant. It was more like formaldehyde with a touch of rot underneath it. Gave me the creeps.

But at least the joint was brightly lit, if with ugly fluorescent lights. Living or dead, or walking dead, no one has ever had their appearance improved by fluorescent lighting.

Greg and I meandered through the hallways between exam rooms and cold storage until we got to Bobby's office. Robert Daniel Reed was not what anyone expected to encounter in a morgue as a medical examiner's assistant. The stereotype of a scrawny little bookworm with visions of defiling corpses flew right out the window when you took a look at Bobby. A former Arena Football League quarterback, he'd migrated from North Georgia when his playing career ended (something about a shot to the knee one night in Birmingham) and tried his hand at entrepreneurial undertaking.

We met Bobby a couple of years ago on a case involving an expensive and prematurely deceased parakeet, and he had become an invaluable resource—a man with an embarrassing bird-related secret in his past and a key to a blood bank. He looked up from what was no doubt a scintillating game of solitaire when we walked in, and his normally cheerful demeanor darkened as soon as he recognized us.

"What do you guys want?" he grumbled, settling all six foot four inches and 260 pounds back into his office chair, which let out a whine of protest.

"I'm hungry, Bobby. What's in the fridge?' Greg walked over to a cooler on the wall.

"Stay out of there, Knightwood, that's a customer."

Greg hastily took his hand off the door handle as Bobby walked over to the wall of slide-out drawers. For a dead guy, Greg has a crazy aversion to corpses. I mean, I'm not a huge fan, but as long as they're lying still, they don't bug me too much. It's when they get up and cause trouble that I have issues.

Bobby reached up and opened a drawer high on the wall, pulling out a sliding steel tray with a pair of Igloo coolers on it. "I keep the stash up here so the boss doesn't get into it."

"Why would that keep him out?" I asked, sitting down at Bobby's computer and updating his Facebook status with stupid movie quotes. That should teach him to leave a window open when there are other people in the room.

"He's five three with lifts in his shoes. He's banned us from ever putting the stiffs in the upper drawers, so I know he can't get into this stuff." Bobby pulled down a cooler and handed it to Greg. "The usual fee?"

"Yeah, here. I put a little extra on here because we're gonna need to fill up before we leave." Greg reached into his utility belt and handed him a thumb drive. Greg's deal with Bobby included not just cash, but cheat codes for the latest Xbox games and some hard-to-find manga.

Bobby stood there looking at us expectantly, and I cocked an eyebrow at him. "You sure you want to watch this? Sometimes people freak out a little."

I wasn't really sure how much Greg had told Bobby about us, so I didn't know if he understood we were the real deal as far as vampires go, or just thought we were humans with a blood fetish. I know, it's gross, but it happens. For that matter, drinking blood grosses *me* out sometimes, and it's how I stay alive.

"Just pretend like I'm not here." Bobby showed no inclination to leave.

I brought a bag up to my lips, grimaced at the cold plastic, and paused as another thought occurred to me. "That's fine, Bobby-boy, but if this shows up on YouTube, my next meal comes straight from the source."

His eyes widened, and he reached over to hit a button on his laptop, apparently turning off the built-in webcam.

Greg and I emptied the cooler, putting away six pints apiece before we ran out of blood, and I felt stronger, faster and even smarter when we were done. Running low on blood always leaves me a little sluggish, but this infusion had me cooking on all eight cylinders again. Even ice-cold and tasting faintly of plastic, a little of the life force of the donor seeped through, and I could smell more sharply, see more clearly and hear more distinctly.

I wiped my mouth with the back of one hand, and then licked the last stray drop from between my fingertips. "Good to the last drop," I murmured, and Greg belched. "You're gross," I chastised my partner.

"It's still funny."

"I didn't say it wasn't funny, just gross. How you doing over there, Bobby?"

Our erstwhile observer had collapsed in his chair and was looking decidedly paler than before we began our meal.

"I-I-I'm okay. I guess. I . . . I . . . just guess I wasn't really sure that you guys were . . ." His voice trailed off, and he looked around, as if to make sure nobody could hear him.

"Vampires?" Greg said from behind him, and giggled as Bobby jumped out of his chair. We're fast, and really quiet when we want to be, and sneaking up on people is one of Greg's favorite and most annoying tricks.

"Yeah. That. So . . . are you guys doing that thing up north?"

Bobby looked at me like I should know what he was talking about, so I played along. "Nah, not this week. We might go back later if the money's right." I had no idea what I had just claimed we did.

"I heard this week's match was really weak. Like the guy didn't even want to be there. Don't know where they get some of these dudes, man. You two would put on a way better show. I hope they call y'all up soon." He made a shadow-boxing motion and gave me two thumbs up.

Boxing? Us? I didn't want to look stupid by asking him to explain now. "Yeah, man. Me too. Hey, if you know anybody who might be able to . . . well, you know, just put a good word in for a loyal customer?" I gave him a business card.

"I'll try. I usually just drive the trucks afterward, you know. But if I get close to the big man I'll try to slip him your card."

"Thanks, Bobby. You rock."

"I know, baby. I know."

"We gotta roll. Later."

"Peace."

I grabbed Greg's elbow and turned him to head out the doors of the morgue and start looking for our gay-basher.

"What was all that about?" Greg asked as we waited for the elevator.

"I have no idea. But it sounds like black market blood isn't the only pie our buddy Bobby has his fingers into, and that might be useful information someday."

Chapter 8

As we drove back to the crime scene, Greg and I started to go over the details of the case. "So what do we know?" I asked, as he turned right onto Hawthorne and put the hospital in the rearview mirror.

"Well, we know that Detective Law has family issues, that some of those issues are currently lying in a hospital bed and that your libido has elected you therapist."

"Bite me," I replied, fiddling with the radio trying in vain to find something other than country music.

"No, thanks, you're stale. But anyway, we know that there have been several of these attacks over the past few months, and the gay community has been up in arms for the police to do more about them. Unfortunately, living as we do in the buckle of the Bible Belt, the police were reluctant to get involved until there had been too many attacks to ignore."

"How do you know so much about this? There hasn't been anything on TV to speak of." I flipped the radio off and stared across the front seat at my partner. "Is there something you've been meaning to tell me?" I teased.

"No, shithead. Popular culture to the contrary, being a vampire is not synonymous with sexual ambiguity. I have not ever been, nor will I ever be attracted to your skinny ass. Or any other part of your undeveloped frame."

"I dunno, Greggy," I needled. "Methinks he doth protest too much."

"Oh, shut up. If I wanted to go after guys, I'd definitely go after better-looking ones than you. But anyway, there's been this invention lately called the Internet. You might have heard of it? I read about the attacks on a couple of city message boards that I monitor."

"What message boards are these, pray tell?" I was beginning to get a sneaking suspicion I knew the answer, but I wanted Greg to admit it.

"Law enforcement message boards. The kinds where people talk about hot spots for crime, places the city can't or won't take care of, that kind of thing. You can find anything on the web if you look hard enough." He looked smug as we pulled into the Spirit Square parking lot and got out of the car.

"Anything except a life, apparently," I muttered as I followed him into the alley.

The crime scene unit had finished up, so we had the run of the place, which was just fine with me. It gave us a chance to use some of our more off-the-record abilities to look over everything. I'd walked the alley a couple of times looking and listening for anything out of the ordinary when I heard Greg give a low whistle. I looked back to see him standing at the top of a concrete staircase leading down to a stage door. He waved me over excitedly, and I headed his way.

"Give this a sniff, dude," he said when I reached him. He pointed at the door.

I leaned over and took a big whiff. My sense of smell is nowhere near as keen as Greg's, but this almost knocked me over. It smelled like rotten food, and blood and serious armpit funk, all overlaid with a coating of cloying floral scent. It was the same as we'd smelled coming off Stephen, only way stronger.

"Ewww. Damn, dude, how about a little warning next time? That is seriously nasty."

"Shut up, you pansy. Have you ever smelled anything like that before?"

"You mean before Stephen's hospital room? No."

"Me neither, but now that I've locked in on it, I can tell it's all over the alley. I think whatever beat up Stephen smelled like this."

"Well, then it oughta be easy to find. Just look for wherever there are a lot of people with sinus trouble, because nobody else could stomach that stench." I saw something fluttering out of the corner of my eye and went back up the stair.

"If you get any of that on your clothes you're totally walking home," Greg yelled after me as I knelt down beside a dumpster and reached under it.

"I'll sit on the roof," I yelled back as I pulled a brightly colored flyer out from under the dumpster. It advertised a drag show at Scorpio, the city's oldest and most famous gay bar. There was a smear of blood across the front of it that told me it had been a lot closer to the fight than it was now, maybe even on Stephen somewhere. I stood up, wiping as much of the alley muck off me as I could. This made the second time tonight that club had come to my attention, and I didn't believe it was coincidence.

I held the flyer out to Greg and said, "Let's get back home and plan our wardrobes."

"For what?" He asked, trying hard to read the flyer and stay downwind of me.

"This show is tomorrow night. We're going clubbing. Now let's get out of here before the sun comes up."

Chapter 9

The next night found me rolling on the floor of my den as Greg trotted out his finest club garb for our investigative trip to the gay bar. I was sporting a patterned T-shirt under a silk blazer with a pair of designer jeans and the only pair of decent shoes I owned, black loafers with buckles. Greg, on the other hand, came out in a pair of black leather pants and a gold mesh shirt that showed far more of my rotund partner than I wanted to know existed.

"Dude," I gasped between howls of laughter, "how many cows had to sacrifice themselves to build those pants? And please don't tell me I'm seeing the sparkle of a belly ring?" I fell off the couch and sat there laughing as Greg stood in the doorway of his room glowering at me.

"Shut up, toothpick. I'm trying to look inconspicuous," he muttered.

"Dude, we're going to a gay bar, not Mardi Gras. You don't have to dress like Captain Jack Sparrow after he slept with a disco ball," I said.

He turned on his heel and went back into his room while I sat there wondering what he would come out with next.

"And since when are you the expert on how to dress for success at a gay bar?" Sabrina asked from the stairs.

I clambered up from the floor and headed over to her. "A guy's gotta eat. How did you get in here? And what are you wearing?" I'd never seen Sabrina in a dress before, and this one didn't leave a whole lot to the imagination. The skirt was short, the top was clingy and red and she had on a pair of heels that I bet were borrowed from a pal in the Vice department.

"One—you're disgusting. Two—you left the door unlocked. And Three—this is called a skirt, and I'm wearing it to the club to keep you two social misfits out of trouble." She went to the fridge and grabbed a beer. "Want one?"

I nodded in the affirmative, and she brought two beers over and set them on the coffee table.

"Judging from Greg's ensemble, it looks like my services will most definitely be needed." She sat down and twisted open a Miller Lite.

"Yeah, we weren't much for the club scene when we were alive, and loud music really plays havoc with our hyper-hearing nowadays, so we don't spend a whole lot of time shaking our groove things." I sat next to her on the couch and propped my feet up. I put my arm along the back of her shoulders, and she didn't shoot me. I took that as a good sign and left my arm there.

"Huh. I hadn't thought about that. How are you going to deal with the noise tonight?" she asked.

"Wax earplugs," I answered. "Greg came up with the idea. They look a little bit like hearing aids but they'll cut enough noise out for us to be able to function. And it's not like I'm looking for a date."

"I thought all of you guys were bi" Sabrina said, looking at me out of the corner of her eye to gauge my reaction.

I didn't give her the satisfaction, just muttered "racist" under my breath and took another sip of my beer. We sat there in easy silence for several seconds. She smelled nice, like lavender with an undertone of spice. I let my hand drop softly onto one shoulder and listened as her heartbeat sped up just a little.

"How's your cousin?" I asked.

"No change. Still unconscious. The doctors don't know why, either. His wounds are pretty bad, but they say he should have woken up by now."

"I'm sorry. We'll find who did this, I promise."

"I know. And thanks. I appreciate everything you're doing."

I tightened my arm around her shoulder in an awkward one-armed hug and just held her. It felt good, then I heard the door to Greg's bedroom creak open, and we jerked apart like guilty teenagers. I smiled at Sabrina, and she gave me a rueful grin in return. I turned to my partner, now resplendent in a flannel shirt and work boots.

"You're a lumberjack and you're okay. Let's go, baby bear," I said, then stood up, and we headed to the car.

We took my car to the club, just in case there was anyone paying attention to the parking lot. Nothing says, "ignore me" like an imported economy car, and we didn't exactly want trumpets announcing our arrival.

The bouncer was wearing a shirt that looked a lot like the one I'd mocked Greg for wearing originally, and he shot me an I-told-you-so look. I didn't bother making any remarks about their respective physiques, just paid the cover and went inside.

It was a good thing Greg had come up with his earplug idea, because I can't stand Lady Gaga at low volume, much less the ridiculous level it was blaring at through the club. The lights were dim everywhere except the dance floor, where the strobes and colored light flashed in time with the music. Everywhere you looked there were ridiculously fit men dancing together, and in the corners of the bar you could see men talking with their heads close together, sometimes holding hands, sometimes just talking. All in all it looked just like a straight dance club only with no women, and I felt just as out of place. Come to think of it, there were never any women in my experience at straight dance clubs either. At least not until they became dinner.

I headed over to the bar and waved the bartender over. He gave me a quick once-over and said "Domestic beer in the bottle?"

"How did you know?"

"It's what all the straight boys drink. It's like a billboard." He smiled and grabbed me three Miller Lites, twisting the tops off into the trash can with a practiced flip of the wrist.

"Who says I'm straight?" I was a little offended that my cover had been blown so quickly.

"Everything about you, sweetie. Don't worry, we don't mind your kind coming in here, just don't start any trouble." He flashed me a smile that I bet got him a lot of second dates, and turned to go down the bar. I waved him over with a couple of twenties, and suddenly his attention was mine and undivided. Some things work with every bartender in the world, no matter the venue, and pictures of Andrew Jackson are a good conversation starter pretty much everywhere.

"Since you know I'm not here looking for a date, I might as well just ask you some questions," I started, but he waved me off right away.

"Sorry, sweetie, not a chance. You've got 'PI' written all over you, and the last thing I need is to end up in some frustrated closet case's divorce hearing."

He started to turn again and I went ahead and brought out the big guns. "I'm investigating the assaults."

He stopped cold and turned back to me. "Really?" He had an eyebrow climbing into his hairline, and I could almost see the wheels turning as he tried to figure out exactly who we were.

"Yeah, really. Our friend in the miniskirt is a CMPD detective, and you were right about my partner and I being private investigators. We're trying to find out more about the victims, and we're starting here."

"Why here? I don't even know a couple of the guys that were beat up, and I know everybody that comes in here more than twice." He looked around and waved the other bartender over. "Come with me. I can't talk to you out here. No. They stay. Just you."

I waved off Sabrina and Greg, and followed him back to the office behind the bar and sat with my back to the door. Not my favorite seating arrangement, but I figured I could out-muscle and out-maneuver anything in a human bar, so I let it slide.

The office was small, but nicely appointed. I was in a nice leather side chair that matched the desk chair pretty perfectly, like it had been part of a set that included the heavy mahogany desk and credenza. Several flat-screen monitors lined the wall to my left, showing various areas of the bar, while certificates and plaques from various charities and arts organizations lined the opposite wall. All in all, it looked a lot like a lawyer's office, if you could ignore the autographed photos of drag queens and Broadway stars that dotted the shelves and walls.

"Alright, what do you want to know?" he asked as he sat behind the desk.

I might not be the sharpest fang in a mouth, but I was starting to get the idea that this guy was more than just a bartender. "Let's start with some introductions. I'm Jimmy. And you are?" I passed him one of my cards, and he tucked it under the corner of a blotter on his desk.

"I'm George. I've been the manager here for the past five years. And I know for a fact that my customers have nothing to do with these attacks."

"And exactly how do you know that?" I asked, turning my chair to at least give myself a little peripheral view of the door.

"Because, like I said out there, some of those guys have never been in here. Or at least have only been in once or twice. They're not regulars, and our regulars are good people. Sure you've got the occasional tweaker and more than the occasional stoner, but most of my boys are just out looking for a good time."

"What if the person doing the attacking was finding his victims here?" I asked. "We don't really think that your establishment has anything to do with the attacks, but a flyer for tonight's drag show was found in the alley at the last attack."

"Well, yeah, it would have been. We papered the hell out of the Spirit Square lot last night. It was kinda our target demographic, you know?"

"No, I don't know. In fact, I have no idea what you're talking about. Help me out a little." I had this sinking feeling in my gut that our best lead so far was going to turn out to be a complete dead end. Sabrina was not going to be happy.

"The play going on at Spirit Square last night?" George went on. "They were doing *Jeffrey*, a total gay comedy. Probably every car in the parking lot belonged to a queen, so I sent one of my bar backs out to put a flyer under all their windshield wipers, so when they came out of the play, they got invited to keep their weekend going here. It's guerilla marketing, baby, the only kind we can afford nowadays. Somebody probably took the flyer off their windshield and tossed it on the ground, then it ended up in the alley."

"Crap. That was our best lead so far."

"Sorry. Wish I could help more, man."

"Yeah, me too. Guess it's time to earn the itty-bitty retainer the CMPD has me on for this case. If you come up with anything else, please let me know." I stood, turning toward the door. I'd just reached my hand out when the door flew open. A twenty-something boy with bleached hair and teeth ran in like the devil himself was outside. Which given my luck, wasn't out of the question.

"George, you gotta come quick. There's this huge guy at the front door and he's fighting with Otto," the boy gasped.

"Otto's a black belt in three different martial arts. I don't think I need to be there to help him." George looked about as concerned as if he'd just been told the floor needed mopping at the end of the night.

"No, you don't understand. He's kicking Otto's ass! We need an ambulance! Call 911, quick!"

The kid was almost hyperventilating, and I shoved past him to get back to the club. I ran past Greg and Sabrina, shouting for them to follow me. We headed to the door at top human speed, still trying to stay under the radar. Any hope of staying incognito flew right out the window when we saw what was waiting for us in the parking lot.

Chapter 10

There was mayhem just outside the front door, and it took me a couple of valuable seconds to figure out exactly what was going on. When I finally got a good look at the scene, I still didn't exactly believe what I was seeing. Otto, the bouncer with Greg's taste in clothing, was bleeding from the nose and mouth and circling a giant on the porch leading to the club's entrance.

Giant is probably a vast oversimplification, but I couldn't come up with a better description for a beast that topped out at about nine feet tall and somewhere in the range of four hundred pounds of solid muscle. This thing had greenish skin, arms bigger around than my waist with claws at the end of each finger and a face that not even a mother could love. Otto was a big dude, and obviously had some hand-to-hand combat chops, because he was still alive, but I knew if we didn't do something fast, that was about to change.

"Do you have a gun hidden somewhere in that outfit?" I asked Sabrina as Greg and I started to fan out and try to flank the giant.

"It's called a handbag, you idiot, and yes," she muttered, knowing she didn't have to speak loudly for me to hear and not wanting to terrify the crowd any more than they already were.

"All right, then get George, the bartender, and tell him what you're going to do." I was moving out of her earshot as I got around behind the beastie.

I saw it freeze and start to sniff the air, and I knew our cover was about to be blown. Vampires have a unique scent, kind of an old blood smell, and creatures that have enhanced senses can pick us out in a heartbeat. That's one reason we don't hunt in the suburbs—too many dogs. This guy obviously had a good sniffer, so our element of surprise was blown. Because it can't ever be easy.

"And what exactly am I going to do?" Sabrina asked.

"Make the crowd ignore this," I yelled as I drew my Glock and leapt for the giant's back.

Greg saw my move and went in from the side at the monster's knees. Otto saw that the cavalry had arrived and launched a flurry of roundhouse kicks at the monster's face to give us a chance to land our best shots.

That didn't go nearly as well as it had in the movie in my mind. The giant took a couple of kicks in the face, but they had about as much effect as peeing on a forest fire. And of course the monster was faster than I expected, so as soon as I landed on its back, it reached over one shoulder and grabbed me by the back of my neck. The thing swept me over its shoulder and right into the path of my flying partner. I crashed into a couple hundred pounds of flying vampire, and my body and my gun flew in opposite directions.

Greg and I thudded to the ground in a tumble of arms, legs and unfortunate wardrobe choices, and I looked up to see a shoe that had to be a size twenty-seven coming down at my head. I flashed back to my fight with Baal a couple of months ago and mentally swore to stop getting stepped on so much.

Greg and I rolled in opposite directions and managed to avoid being stomped into paste. We got up on opposite sides of the creature. I kicked the thing in the knee, and it backhanded me off the porch into the parking lot. I skidded through the gravel for several feet before coming to a halt against a BMW convertible. I struggled to my feet and leaned against a dent in the fender, thinking about all the *Twilight* jokes I was going to have to listen to over that one.

Greg was standing toe-to-toe with the monster, landing huge haymakers on the monster's midsection. I thought I heard a rib crack, and the thing reared back in pain. Then it lashed out with a foot and caught Greg square in the gut. He flew several feet through the air and landed right behind me in the windshield of the Beamer.

I pulled him free of the shattered glass and said, "You okay?"

"No. You?"

"Not really. Let's go."

With that, we ran back at the monster, Greg going low for its knees while I went for a flying clothesline. The thing just jumped straight up into the air, making Greg miss entirely and swatting me out of the air like a wobbly Frisbee. Which is how I landed, too. I got to my feet, wiped a little blood out of my face, and circled around to the monster's side. Greg went in the opposite direction, and to my surprise, Otto the bouncer flew in with a dropkick that rocked the thing back on its heels.

He landed in front of the monster in a combat stance, ready to throw down, if a little unsteady on his feet.

"Get out of here," I growled at the bouncer. "You're just gonna get killed."

"Not tonight, friend. But I do appreciate your assistance," the bouncer replied. Then he made an odd gesture with his right hand. Suddenly a gleaming sword with a three-foot blade appeared out of thin air, and Otto launched himself at the giant, sword raised high above his head. He moved almost faster than I could see, and that's really saying something.

"I hate surprises in the middle of a fight," I muttered, dropping to one knee under a backhanded blow from the giant. While I was on one knee I pulled my backup pistol from an ankle holster and emptied the clip into the giant's crotch.

The beast screamed in pain, and Otto's sword flashed down lightning-quick, cleaving the monster's head from its shoulders and splattering greenish-black blood all over Otto, Greg and me. I licked my lips experimentally, but apparently giant blood has no nutritional value, so I was just grossed out.

"Ick," Greg said, wiping giant blood and whatever else out of his eyes.

"Ick indeed," I agreed, looking around for Sabrina.

The porch, which had been crowded with onlookers just seconds before, was curiously empty. Only the four of us and the corpse of a green-blooded behemoth were outside the club. I looked over to where Sabrina was leaning against the closed door of the club and asked, "What did you do?"

She smiled back at me and said, "I held up my badge and gun and shouted 'Raid!' as loud as I could. You'd be amazed how many guys are flushing little baggies of things down the toilet right now. But you probably still want to clean this mess up pretty quickly. And put that away." She pointed at the glowing sword Otto was holding.

He waved it in another curious gesture, and the blade disappeared.

"That was effective. You wanna tell us exactly what the hell is going on here?" I asked the bouncer.

"No, but that probably isn't an option, is it?"

"No. It's not."

"Okay, then. Help me get this mess out of here before anybody notices, then we can go somewhere and I'll explain everything."

"All right. What do you drive, because there's no way this beast is gonna fit in my Camry."

"I've got a truck. I'll bring it around," Otto said as he started off toward the parking lot.

"Way to buck the stereotype," I said to his back as I started picking up arms and legs, trying to figure out how we were going to get the monster into the back of a pickup.

Otto just flipped me off without looking back, then went around the building toward what I assumed was the employee parking lot. He came back a few minutes later in a small panel truck with the club logo painted on the side, and backed it expertly up to the corpse. He jumped out and grabbed the beast under the arms. With a strength that belied his human appearance, he picked up the creature's torso and stood there staring at Greg and me.

"You two going to help me, or do I have to do everything?" he asked.

We each grabbed a thigh and together we wrestled the giant into the truck. Otto tossed the head in beside the body, slammed the door down and said, "I'll take care of this. Meet me at Landmark in two hours." Without looking to see if I had any objections, he got into the driver's seat and pulled out of the parking lot.

"I don't think I want to know what he's going to do with a headless giant in Charlotte at 2 A.M. on a Saturday night," I said as I headed down the hill to my car.

"Yeah," Greg agreed, squelching along beside me, oozing monster blood with every step. "And I don't want to know how much it's going to cost to clean your upholstery after this ride home."

Chapter 11

After a quick trip home to clean up and contemplate burning our clothes, Greg, Sabrina and I headed to The Landmark, a twenty-four-hour restaurant famous for decent food and interesting atmosphere, especially after hours. Greg and I were in our more normal garb, while Sabrina was still in her club wear. I'd offered her some of my clothes, but apparently *Sandman* T-shirts and sweatpants were not her style.

We took a booth in the back and waited for Otto to arrive. He made it there before our drinks did, dressed down in a long-sleeved polo and a baseball cap over his bald pate. He'd obviously taken the time to shower as well, because there wasn't a hint of slimy green blood anywhere on him. The waiter took our orders, and then went off to leave us to our conversation.

"Okay, Otto. Let's start by telling us what that thing was? It looked like a giant with bad hygiene," I started.

"No, that wasn't a giant. It wouldn't have come up to a giant's belt buckle. That was a troll," the bouncer-turned-troll-slayer said matter-of-factly. The waiter paused for a second in delivering our drinks, then shrugged and set the glasses on the table. I guess he'd heard a lot weirder stuff.

"Just once, I'd like to meet a supernatural creature that couldn't spot us from fifty yards away. Just once," Greg muttered from across the booth.

"I pegged you two from a hundred yards away as vampires. It took the other fifty yards to peg you as straight boys," Otto said.

"Anyway," I interrupted, not interested in yet another conversation about the general sexual preferences of vampires, "that doesn't answer the question of what the troll was doing there. Got any ideas, or did you just slice first and ask questions later?"

"I didn't ask. Trolls are ancient enemies of my people. The mere sight of one in my city filled me with an uncontrollable rage, and I attacked. I lost control of myself, bringing shame to my father and my House."

I had no idea what he was talking about. "Who are your people?" I asked, figuring I'd start slow.

"The Fae. Your people call us faeries," he said.

"I know that, but Greg and I, we're a little more progressive than that. We believe in live and let live, don't ask don't tell, whatever two consenting adults do is between them, that whole thing." I trailed off weakly when I saw him looking at me like I was a moron. I get that look often enough to recognize it, unfortunately.

"Not homosexuals, vampire. Faeries. Like in the tales. Except we don't all have wings, and we're not tiny. As you can see." As if to prove a point, he stood up and struck a pose like a Greek statue.

"I get it, I get it. Now sit down," I hissed. He sat, and I leaned forward. "Now, you say you're a real faerie, like faerie godmother faerie?"

"Yes, although I have no intention of singing bibbity-bobbity-boo with you."

"And you guys hate trolls and trolls hate faeries?"

"Yes."

"But how does something like that move around a city unnoticed? It was nine friggin' feet tall if it was an inch. And it was uglier than Greg going through Xbox withdrawal." I knocked back my Coke and motioned to the waiter for another.

"Glamour," Otto said simply.

"Gonna need a little more, babe. I don't think you're hiding that much ugly with Cover Girl concealer," Sabrina said.

"No, human." Otto managed to make "human" sound a lot like "cockroach," but I let it slide. Besides, the term didn't technically apply to me anymore. "Magic. Creatures of the higher realms can easily manipulate what is seen by those from more mundane planes."

"So the troll used magic to hide its true nature until it started fighting you?" I asked, starting to get the picture.

"Yes, then it needed all its resources just to survive. But all those resources weren't quite enough." His face split in a nasty smile, and for a second I was very happy that he hadn't turned that magical sword in my direction.

"This is going to sound like a stupid question, but what is a faerie doing working the door at a gay bar?" I asked. Sometimes I can't believe the words that come out of my own mouth.

"I was sent here to find out who is attacking my people. There have been several attacks on the Fae who live in this city. Our queen sent me here to put a stop to it. Even if they choose to live in this mundane world, her people are still under her protection."

"Your people?" Sabrina asked. "Are you telling me some of the victims of these attacks are faeries?"

"Not some," Otto said. "All of the victims so far have been of the Fae."

"The bloodstains on the wall where Stephen was attacked would be consistent with marks left by a troll attack," Greg observed, moving his waffles around so it looked like he was eating.

"My cousin isn't a faerie, at least not in the literal sense of the word. No offense." She nodded to Otto.

"None taken. But may I ask, what is your cousin's name?"

"Stephen Neal. He's a dancer."

"Hmmm." The faerie looked at Sabrina, then at his drink, then back at Sabrina, then back at his drink.

"It's still full. Now spit it out," Sabrina said, slamming her open hand down on the table.

The faerie looked at her and smiled. "I like you. You are strong for one of the mundane world. You would make a good faerie. Like your cousin. He is not who you think he is. Or what."

Sabrina sat there for a moment staring at Otto, then drained her soda in one long gulp. She waved the waiter over and ordered a screwdriver, light on the OJ, and downed that before responding. We all looked on in silence as she leaned in, took hold of the front of Otto's shirt and pulled him close.

She spoke very slowly and distinctly, as if she were having trouble with the language. "Now. What were you saying about my cousin?"

Otto looked around, made sure that there were no civilians nearby, then pried Sabrina's hand from his shirt. She winced, but let go. "Stephen isn't really your cousin. At least not by any blood relation. He's one of us. Your legends call him a changeling. In certain cases we switch faerie children with human newborns, taking the human child to our lands and leaving the faerie babe to be raised as human."

"Why?" Greg asked.

Sabrina looked stunned, like she didn't know what to say.

Otto fidgeted for a minute, but eventually answered after another glare from Sabrina. "Sometimes it's because the human infant has a condition that could prove fatal without treatments that aren't available in human society, sometimes it's because the family situation of the child is unfavorable, and sometimes . . ." Otto trailed off and I saw Sabrina's eyes go hard.

"Sometimes?" she prodded.

I knew that look, and really hoped Otto wouldn't pick this moment to get stubborn. I wasn't sure the furnishings could survive a clash of wills. And I couldn't afford any more demolished wardrobe tonight.

"Sometimes we need the children to breed with our children to keep a particular line alive. The Fae do not reproduce as quickly as humans do, but we can breed with humans if need be. Our numbers have dwindled in recent centuries, and we occasionally have to resort to extraordinary measures to insure our survival."

"Extraordinary measures?" Sabrina asked.

This conversation was going sideways fast, and I waved the waiter over for our check. I shoved Greg out of the booth to go pay at the counter before my friend and the faerie bouncer redecorated the restaurant in Early Apocalypse.

"Why don't we relocate this conversation somewhere a little more private?" I asked. "We're starting to draw a little attention, and that could be unfortunate for everyone involved."

"Where would you suggest, vampire?" Otto asked.

"Our place, and go easy on the 'vampire' stuff, Tinkerbelle. Some of us try to stay incognito." I got up and headed for the door, Sabrina and Otto followed exchanging glances like two cats that you just know are going to start fighting the second you put the Fancy Feast down. "Greg will ride with you and show you the way," I said to Otto over my shoulder. I led Sabrina out the front door to my car.

The ride to our place was uneventful, mostly because Sabrina sulked the whole way. The way she was acting, you'd think she wanted to tussle with a supernatural beefcake in the middle of a twenty-four-hour diner. We went down the stairs into the apartment (because I hate to think of it as a crypt, regardless of the fact that it sits underneath a cemetery, and besides, crypts don't have high-speed Internet) and got a couple of beers out of the fridge. Then I called in the cavalry, or more specifically, Father Mike. Mike had been running interference at the hospital since we left Stephen there, but I figured his calming influence and priest's collar might be needed.

Greg and Otto got to our place a few minutes after Sabrina and I opened our beers, and we all settled into the living room. Greg pulled a chair over from the computer for himself while Otto sat in the armchair.

I stationed myself on the arm of the couch next to where Sabrina sat, putting myself between her and Otto, in hopes that I could calm them down if it all went pear-shaped.

Sabrina took a long pull of her beer and looked over at Otto. "I believe you were about to explain how you kidnap human babies and use them for breeding stock, weren't you?" Her voice could have been coated in honey, except for the obvious razor blade hidden underneath her tone.

"That is a crude way of putting things, but true enough at the root of it all. We did in fact replace your female cousin with a child of our own, the boy that grew up to be your cousin Stephen. No harm has ever been done to the girl, who lives among our people as one of us, and has risen to a certain prominence within our House." Otto paused for a drink, and I took a second to evaluate how Sabrina was handling this news.

She looked shell-shocked, to say the least. "A girl? Stevie was supposed to be a girl?"

"Yes. The child we replaced was a female. We have no real need of human males. It is the gestation cycles of our women that are at issue, not the libido of our men." Otto actually blushed at this, as though this was something not usually discussed in polite company.

Good thing for him he wasn't in polite company.

Of course, this was when Mike made his appearance, which was good, because I needed an excuse to get another drink.

"Hello, boys. What's the emergency?" Mike asked as he came down the stairs and tossed his overcoat on the back of a kitchen chair. I'd given a little thought to a coat rack, but it would just be another thing to not ever get used, kinda like Greg's NordicTrack. I've gotta tell you, that was one disappointed vampire when he realized that no matter how much he worked out, he was never going to burn any fat. Being stuck in the body you died in might be good for Brad Pitt, but when you're an overweight twenty-something, and you're going to be fat for eternity, it just sucks.

I met Mike over by the bar and poured him a double scotch. He took one look at the glass and raised an eyebrow. "That bad?"

I just held out the drink, and he downed it. I poured him another and brought him over to the sofa. He sat next to Sabrina, and I reclaimed my perch on the arm.

I made the requisite introductions and caught Mike up to speed on where we were in the story. It's a credit to how long he's been hanging around with vampires that he barely raised an eyebrow until we got to the changeling bits. Then he stopped me.

"Jimmy, my boy, are you telling me that these . . . faeries . . . steal human girls and use them for brood mares?"

Sometimes I forget that even though Greg and I went to Clemson, Mike actually spent summers on a farm in his youth.

"I think that's about where we had gotten to when you walked in, Padre." Sabrina had managed to stay quiet through my retelling of the night's events, but I could tell she was seething. Part of it was the pulse I could hear pounding in her veins, but mostly it was the I-want-to-eat -someone's-liver tone of voice she was using.

Otto raised a hand to interrupt. "If I may explain?"

I nodded at him, really hoping that he had something good up his sleeve. "The girls are raised as our own, and with the rarity of children in our Houses, they are revered beyond measure. There is good reason every little human girl dreams of being a Faerie Princess, after all." Otto smiled a knowing smile at Sabrina, who bristled at the condescension.

"Some little girls dream of being the ones off slaying dragons, you pointy-eared chauvinist. And regardless, there's a difference between a Faerie Princess and a prostitute. You can't just go around taking little girls and replacing them with faerie boys."

"But what if the little girls would never grow up healthy in your world?" Otto asked mildly.

"What are you talking about?" Sabrina growled.

"Your cousin had a rare genetic disorder called Tay-Sachs disease that would have killed her in childhood had she remained here, probably before she entered kindergarten. By taking her to our lands, we were able to use magic to heal her and allow her to live a normal, if pampered, life."

"Then why didn't you bring her back when she was healed? Why don't you just come over here and heal all the sick babies? Why are you only so magnanimous to the ones you want to squeeze out litters of little faeries for you?" Sabrina wasn't ready to let this one go yet.

"Much faerie magic only exists within the boundaries of our realm. If you bring faerie coin into your world, the gold turns to lead. If you take faerie food out of Faerie, it turns to dust within minutes. And if your cousin were to return to the mundane world, the changes wrought upon her body would immediately reverse, and she would die a horrible, painful death. So she is forced to live in the lands of the Fae and be treated like a precious treasure instead of coming back here to die in agony. Does that sound like a fair enough trade?" Otto leaned back in the chair and sipped his beer while Sabrina tried to process this new information.

"I guess so," she said after a long moment.

She got up from the couch, headed over to the bar and poured herself a stiff drink. She drank down half of her drink and came back to where we were all watching her expectantly. I tensed, ready to throw myself between Sabrina and the faerie if bullets started to fly.

She took a deep breath and said, "Okay, you and Stevie are faeries. You killed a troll at Scorpio because trolls are sworn enemies of faeries, and all the evidence points to a troll attacking Stevie in the alley. Now what?"

"What do you mean, now what?" Otto asked.

"Is that the only troll in Charlotte, or are there more?" Sabrina asked. "And why did a troll beat up my cousin? And why have other gay men been attacked all over town? Are they all faeries? Have all of these been troll attacks? And if so, why? And where do we go to find out?" Her voice had been steadily rising with each question until it was high and thready by the end. I could tell that the night had taken a toll on her, but nothing prepared me for what I heard next.

Otto stood up and put a hand on her shoulder. She looked at him, and the bald faerie said something I thought I'd never hear outside of a Disney movie.

"We must journey to the lands of the Fae."

Chapter 12

The first words out of my mouth were pretty predictable, I suppose. I looked Otto in the eye and said, "Are you out of your addled little mind? There's no such thing as Faerieland, and even if there was, there's no way we're going there. Tell him, Greg."

I looked over at my partner, but he had a look on his face that was somewhere between "kid at Christmas" and "teenager just got to second base."

"I'm up for a trip to Faerieland, bro. Let's roll." He actually bounced off the couch to his feet.

Otto looked down at Sabrina. "We must journey to Faerie to save your cousin. From what Greg told me of his injuries, he has been wounded by a *blanthron*, a spiked glove favored by Trollish gladiators. The spikes are often tipped with venom from the *verdirosa* plant, the Green Rose. It is an extremely dangerous plant that grows only in Faerie."

"And you know all this from Greg talking about Stephen's injuries?" I crossed my arms and stared at the faerie, not buying any of it.

"No, I know this because nothing else in all the realms, magic or mundane, smells like *verdirosa* venom. A floral scent, with a hint of death underneath."

"You win. Whatever beat up Stephen had faerie poison on his fists. Gee, kids! There's a faerie in my living room. First one I've ever met. Guess who's my chief suspect?"

I tried to loom over Otto, but he stood up. He was a lot more buff than me, and having seen him fight, I knew he could probably take me. So I put a Glock in his face to even the odds.

"Sit down, Tink."

Otto sat. "I did not harm Stephen. As a Knight-Mage of House Armelion, I am sworn to protect him. He is my charge, my duty."

"My cousin. My family," Sabrina said from beside me. Her Smith & Wesson service pistol wasn't pointed at Otto, but it was out and ready.

"Can't we all calm down and discuss this logically?" Mike said.

He put a hand on Sabrina's shoulder, pushing her gently back to the sofa. Then he moved in front of me, putting his face in my line of fire. I lowered my gun. This was not the night to be shooting my friends in the face. Not with more appealing targets right there in the room. I sat back down on the arm of the couch.

"Good," Mike said. "Now, let's question our friend Otto, shall we?" He turned to the faerie, put his hand on his cross and rested the other hand on the bald man's forehead and said "Do you swear in the sight of God to tell me the truth?"

"I am of the Fae, minister. I cannot lie. It is not in my nature," Otto replied.

"Yeah, I read that somewhere," Greg said.

"Greg, that was an Alex Craft novel. It wasn't exactly a scholarly work." I pointed to his copy of *Grave Witch* on an end table.

Greg had fallen in love with the author when he saw her picture on a website. I didn't blame him. Blue-haired chicks in corsets are hot. But they are not necessarily reliable primary research sources.

"Regardless, I am incapable of lying directly," Otto said. "Ask me anything, I must tell you the truth or not answer at all."

"Did you harm Stephen Neal?" Mike asked.

"No. From the information Greg gave me, I would guess that he was attacked by a troll wearing poisoned *blanthrons*."

"Will he recover?" Sabrina asked.

"Not without an antivenin prepared from the leaves and roots of the *verdirosa* plant," Otto said.

"Which only grows in Faerieland." I really didn't want to go to Faerieland.

"Correct," Otto replied.

"What happens to Stephen if he doesn't get this antivenin?" Sabrina asked.

"He will die. Depending on the exposure, he has three or four days to live without treatment."

"Crap. Then I guess we go to Faerieland," I said. "Just one question. How do we get there?"

"I am a Knight-Mage of the Fae, and I can grant us passage into the lands of House Armelion," Otto said.

He waved his arms and a brilliant golden glow surrounded him. I turned away from the bright lights, and when I looked back at him he was standing in front of my couch wearing golden chain mail and a helmet. The sword that he conjured up in the troll fight was strapped across his back with the hilt poking over one shoulder, and he looked nothing like the human bouncer that had stood in my den a few seconds before. He looked alien somehow, like his features were just a little too angular, his eyes just a little too blue to be real. And his ears had tapered to distinct points. I also noticed a hint of fang when he spoke, so it looked like Greg and I weren't the only ones vying to be top of the food chain.

"How did you do that?" Sabrina asked, gaping at him.

"My human appearance was a glamour. This is my true self." He smiled, as if he knew how ridiculously good-looking he was, and I started to feel a little self-conscious. I marched over to the coat closet and grabbed my shoulder rig and duster and started arming up.

"Trolls can do that? The glamour thing?" Greg asked.

"Yes," Otto replied. "That is how they manage to pass among humans without notice. They appear to be nothing more than boorish, overweight humans that smell bad."

"So you mean like the typical American," Mike said wryly. I noticed that he was seated at Greg's computer.

"You not coming with us, Dad?" I asked.

"No, Jimmy, I think an excursion to Faerieland might be pushing the bounds of my ordination a little too far. I'll stay here and consult my sources to any information we can find on this side of the veil about trolls and faeries," he answered with a wave to the computer.

"In other words, you're going to hang out with the cute witch that has an unreasoning bias against vampires," Greg observed.

Our priestly friend at least had the good grace to blush slightly. "I will indeed be visiting my Wiccan friend, and you must admit that a human's fear of vampires isn't exactly unreasoning. You do look upon us as a source of nutrition, after all. I'll also stop by the hospital tomorrow morning and see how your cousin is doing, Sabrina."

With that, Mike finished his drink and headed upstairs, moving a little more slowly than I remembered. I looked after him a little worriedly. Mike had taken a couple of tough shots in our last big fight, and my friend's mortality was fresh in my mind. I was honestly a little relieved that he wouldn't be joining us on this trip. I had enough on my plate looking after Sabrina and making sure that Greg didn't fall in love with a faerie girl.

I finished gearing up and walked over to Otto. "All right, Mr. Spock, how do we do this?"

He either ignored or didn't get my Star Trek reference and said, "First, you must all remove anything made of iron or steel that you have on your persons, including your guns."

I held both hands in the air and protested, "Oh hell no. You want me to go into a magical wonderland and meet with fantastical creatures on their home turf, and now you want me to do it unarmed? You gotta be nuts, baldy."

"This is not a point of discussion, vampire. Cold iron is lethal to my people, and to carry it into a meeting is a grave insult. You may bring weapons of bronze, or silver, but no iron or steel can be on your persons." Otto crossed his arms and stared at me stubbornly.

I looked at Sabrina and Greg for support, but all I saw was two people busily divesting themselves of any metal.

"What about zippers?" Greg asked, pointing to the crotch of his jeans.

"Modern jeans use brass or aluminum zippers, so they're fine," Otto replied.

I took a look at Sabrina's nightclub ensemble and figured that wouldn't be the best thing for traipsing around a magical kingdom picking poisonous plants in, so I grabbed a spare pair of sweats for her out of my bedroom, along with the *Sandman* T-shirt she'd declined earlier, and she went into the bathroom to change.

I found a belt that I remembered had a solid titanium Batman belt buckle (don't ask), and loaded a pair of matching silver daggers into it. I poked around my room for a minute and found a tall staff I'd bought at a Ren Faire back before I turned. I slipped on a pair of black leather gloves to let me handle the silver daggers without any adverse effects, and I was ready to rock. Greg found a nightstick and a pair of brass knuckles, and when Sabrina came out of the bathroom I passed her a baseball bat I kept in the closet. All in all we looked like a cross between a demented sports team and the Fellowship of the Ring.

"Okay, Otto, let's go see the faeries," I said when we were all suitably, if ridiculously, attired.

"Before we go," he replied, "I should tell you something of our land. We will attempt to meet with Milandra, the Queen of House Armelion. There may be challenges set for us before we are allowed into her presence, to prove our worth. You must not protest these challenges, or you may be killed outright. Ours is an old society, much older than any human civilization, and our traditions are strong. We are a long-lived people, and change is slow to come to the Fae. We are not like humans, who change with the direction of the wind."

I noticed that Otto's speech had changed as he got closer to going home. He started to sound a lot more like one of Tolkien's elves and less like the bouncer at a gay bar in North Carolina.

"I get it," I said. "Don't piss off the faeries, they'll kick my ass. Now can we move this party along? I'd like to be there and back again before daylight. I didn't pack my sunscreen."

"Very well, vampire. I can see that you will simply have to experience this for yourself. Please remember, stay close to me and try, please try, to keep your mouth shut." With that, he made some kind of hoodoo gesture in the air, and a shimmering portal of light appeared in my living room. "Step through, each of you. I will hold the portal here and follow."

"I just hope that thing doesn't stain my carpet," I said, and stepped through the hole in the air to Faerieland.

Chapter 13

I stepped through the glowing yellow circle and right out the other side. I could tell immediately that I wasn't in Kansas, or North Carolina, anymore. For one thing, the sky was a pale pink with fluffy purple clouds. For another thing, it was daylight, and I wasn't bursting into flames. I got out of the way as Sabrina and Greg came through and looked around. Otto followed close behind them and made some hand gestures that closed the portal behind us.

"It looks like a My Little Pony convention in here," Greg said.

"If anyone would recognize one, it's you." I looked over at Otto. "Why aren't we on fire? It's daylight, and we're outside. We should be crispy critters by now."

Otto looked at me like I was an idiot and said, "You're in the HomeLands, vampire. The sunlight cannot harm you here unless the queen deems it so. Do you understand nothing of your nature?"

"My nature?" I asked. "I'm a vampire. I'm fast, strong, and if I follow a few simple rules I'll never die. I stay out of the sun, avoid big toothpicks and decapitation, and I have a few dietary restrictions. What else is there to understand?"

"I was right. You understand nothing. Let it suffice to say that because you are magical in nature, the light of a magical realm cannot harm you. Anything else is not my place to say. But you should seek some insight into the nature of your existence, vampire. You cannot live forever without sometimes peering inwards."

"Yeah, yeah, 'the unexamined life is not worth living' and all that. But the point is, we're made from magic and the sunlight here won't kill us." I looked around at the foliage in a rainbow of colors. Orange plants, purple grass, blue clover, the whole place was starting to remind me of a bowl of Lucky Charms.

"Correct. A vast oversimplification, but it is correct. Now, we must make our way to the Hall of Queen Milandra." Otto started off down a trail that I hadn't even noticed before, a beaten track of yellow earth between two tall trees that looked like pines, only with pink and green needles.

"How long is that going to take? We're on a little bit of a deadline here," Sabrina reminded him.

"It depends on how long you stand there, and how quickly you start moving," Otto called back to us.

I started after him, struggling through the undergrowth. As I was fighting with one particularly thorny bush, I heard Greg ask, "What's up with the Technicolor foliage? It looks like somebody's TV needs the color calibrated."

"I think it's pretty," Sabrina replied, and looking back at her I saw a strange look on her face. She looked at peace somehow, and younger. It's like I was getting a glimpse of the girl she used to be, before she had to become the tough police detective.

"Our queen has unique tastes in décor, and the realm reflects her desires. Please follow closely. There are things off the paths in Faerie that do not take kindly to visitors," Otto said as he continued to break a trail ahead of us.

He didn't so much cut a path as wave his sword at the undergrowth, and it pulled back enough for us to pass, mostly. Except that the little sticker plants seemed to take a particular glee in poking me in the ass as I walked by. After one particularly sharp jab, I turned around and cut the plant off near the ground with my silver dagger. The stalk hissed and bubbled when I sliced through it with the dagger, and I heard a high-pitched keening wail that sounded as though it came from far away. Otto immediately turned and strode back to where I was standing, sticker plant in hand.

"What are you doing? I told you to stay close," he snapped.

I held the plant up to him and shook it.

He blanched at the sight of it and snatched it away from me. Then he flung the plant into the woods and leaned in close to my face. "Do you *want* to die here, you idiot? Do not attack creatures here. You don't know what they are and you have no idea what they can do to you."

"Otto, it's a plant."

"No, it isn't a plant. That was, for lack of a better word, a finger. A finger of a *terranthyl*, a creature with a plant-like form that attacks by first separating its prey from a group, then dragging the poor creature off into the woods to be devoured. And now you've made it angry. Stay by my side. The *terranthyl* will not attack a Knight-Mage.

I kept close to Otto after that, and tried not to look appetizing. We walked for about three miles before the trees parted and we came into a clearing. Or at least I thought it was a clearing at first. When I continued to look around, I realized that the buildings were so carefully integrated into the forest as to appear that they belonged there. A doorway looked more like a natural crack in a rock face, a chimney looked more like a spire of dead tree and windows just looked like extra knotholes in a tree trunk. The houses were so cleverly disguised that unless you knew what you were looking at, you could walk right through the clearing and never have any idea you'd just passed through the heart of town. Otto led us to the base of an enormous tree that I normally would have called an oak, except I've never seen a pink and purple paisley oak tree before. We walked up a slight ramp that wound around the tree to a crack in the trunk about eight feet off the ground, where he stopped, removed his helmet and knocked.

As we waited, Otto looked at me and said, "Please try to be respectful. Milandra is a kind and gentle queen, but she is the absolute ruler here. Her every whim is answered, not just by we who serve her, but by the very land itself."

"What makes you think I wouldn't be respectful?" I asked, feeling a little insulted. Sabrina glared at me, and I shut up.

After a minute or two of waiting, the door opened, and we stepped into the greatest great hall I'd ever seen. The floor was pink marble, shot through with veins of lavender, pale blue and flecks of white. The ceiling, which must have been thirty feet above us, was painted (or magicked) into looking just like the sky outside, only this was an earthly blue sky with white clouds. There were even birds flying across, which gave me even more reason to believe there was magic involved.

The walls were cut from even more marble, fading slowly from the pink of the floor to the sky blue as they went up. And at the far end of the hall, at least a football field away, stood a twenty-foot dais with a throne on it surrounded by ladies in waiting. A double column of armored knights lined the hall leading to the throne, and every faerie in the honor guard made Otto look like the "before" pic in one of those old Charles Atlas ads from the back of a comic book. They looked at us with undisguised contempt, and I suddenly really, really wanted my guns.

On the throne sat Milandra, and if there was an encyclopedia entry for "regal," she'd be the illustration. Tall, blonde and beautiful, with high cheekbones and delicate features, she was everything Hollywood dreamed of when making a Faerie Queen.

Chapter 14

We got to the foot of the dais, and Otto poked me in the back again. "Kneel," he said, doing so himself.

I went to one knee and out of the corner of my eye saw Sabrina and Greg doing the same.

"Rise, Octavian. And please, introduce us to your guests. Two of the Sanguine and a human? You have selected strange companions, Knight-Mage." Queen Milandra's voiced poured over us like honey, but I could tell that there was a bee sting in there somewhere from the way Otto stiffened.

He bowed his head again and answered, "Your Majesty, may I introduce Detective Sabrina Law, a Peacekeeper of her realm, and her lieutenants, James and Gregory, of the Sanguine."

"It is our pleasure to meet you, Lady Law, and your servants."

I stopped thinking how adorable she was when she got to the bit about servants. I drew in a breath to correct the little Faerie Princess, but Otto shot me another warning look. I shut up, but I was getting a little tired of biting my tongue in the name of interspecies relations.

"Thank you for receiving us, Your Majesty," Sabrina said, stepping forward with a curtsy. She made a warning gesture to me behind her back, and I kept my mouth shut. Now I knew we were in a different dimension, because no way in hell was Sabrina ever going to curtsy to anyone.

"You are welcome here, Lady. Please treat the Great Hall of Armelion as your home for as long as you require our hospitality."

I saw Otto relax when she said that, and I hoped that meant she'd just pledged that no one in her court would try to stake me as long as we were here.

"Many thanks, Your Majesty." Sabrina curtsied again, and I heard Gloria Steinem's ghost screaming in feminist agony somewhere across the dimensional void.

"Octavian, do you pledge the good behavior of our guests and that they mean no harm to our royal person?" the queen asked Otto.

He stood up straighter, if that's possible for someone who was already making a marine at parade rest look like a slinky, and said, "I do, Your Majesty. Upon my honor as Knight-Mage of House Armelion, they shall bring no harm to your person or House."

"Fair enough, Otto, fair enough."

With that, Queen Milandra waved a hand, and the honor guard all disappeared, along with most of the great hall, leaving behind only two guards and a much smaller sitting room. The guards took up positions beside the door, while Greg and I gaped at the new room. I heard tinkling laughter, and spun around to see Milandra sitting, not on a throne, but on what looked like a very comfy armchair, laughing at our confusion.

"Oh, I do love visitors!" She exclaimed with glee. "Especially visitors from the mundane world. Your faces are absolutely priceless." She waved us over to a pair of sofas that had appeared when the room changed. "I prefer to hold audience for friends in my chambers. The great hall is just so drafty this time of year, and no matter how I make the weather outside, it always seems to be chilly in there. I suppose it's all the marble, but I can't remake the great hall, you know."

I sat on the sofa furthest from the queen and closest to the door, not just to keep my escape clear, but also in case something that didn't like me came through the door. Not that I had a lot of hope of taking out anything that could get past the kind of magic Milandra was throwing around, but it made me feel better. "Your Majesty," I began, "We need your help—"

She cut me off with a wave of her hand and turned to Sabrina. "Who let him speak? And why did you let him keep his tongue in the first place? Have you not heard of their powers of persuasion? Or do you just find it exciting to tempt fate?" Her eyes sparkled with the last question, as though tempting fate was one of her favorite pastimes.

"He speaks whenever he pleases, sometimes much to my chagrin. And regardless, his tongue would just grow back if I removed it," Sabrina said, nodding politely to the serving girl who had just brought out a tray of drinks and fruit.

She took a small glass with a pale orange liquid in it, but didn't drink immediately. The queen took a small plate of fruit and a pale lavender drink for herself, then waved over another serving girl, who knelt at Greg's feet, looking up at him with a small smile.

"Do you thirst, vampire? You may drink of Tirina if you wish. But please, leave enough for your friend to share, and do not drain her or I will be very cross." I heard steel in the queen's words, and decided I didn't want to see her cross. Greg looked at Milandra like she was absolutely insane, and started to shake his head.

"Drink, you idiot," I whispered to him. "You don't know when you'll have the chance to feed again, and I doubt there's a blood bank anywhere near here."

"But dude," Greg whispered back plaintively. "I don't do that anymore. I haven't drunk from a person in almost ten years. I can't do it now, in front of people." He got really quiet on the last part, like he was talking about losing his virginity or peeing in public or something.

"You have to, bro. You've gotta keep your strength up, and I know you didn't eat anything before we left the house. Plus, I don't want to piss her off by not accepting." I really didn't want to start some kind of inter-dimensional diplomatic incident by not drinking the girl. Besides, I wanted a snack and had never had faerie for lunch before.

"Your friend is right, vampire. You must drink. I can sense your hunger," Milandra said.

I looked over at the little queen, and she wasn't smiling anymore. She looked at Greg like he was something she wanted to scrape off the bottom of her shoe.

Greg noticed. He stared at the girl's neck for another moment, then took a deep breath and leaned in. He got close enough to brush the faerie girl's neck with his fangs, then pulled back.

"I can't. I *don't* do that." He stood up and turned to me, his jaw set.

"My Lady, are you not in control of your servants? If you would like some assistance in teaching them manners, we would be happy to oblige." The queen's words belied her light tone, and I looked at the guards, trying to decide if I could take them. Maybe, but not Otto.

I put a hand on Greg's shoulder and looked him in the eye. He tried to turn away, but I didn't let him. "Greg, you gotta drink. I know it's a big deal to you, and I'm sorry. *Really* sorry. But either you feed off this girl, or we have to fight our way out of here, and Sabrina's cousin is probably going to die. Now it's up to you."

"I just don't want to lose control again," he whispered.

I looked around, but nobody but me had heard him. "You won't. I won't let you. You'll never be that guy again. I swear it."

There were red-tinged tears in his eyes as he looked up at me. "You promise? This is the last time?"

How could he ask me something like that? I didn't know what was going to happen in the next five minutes, much less the whole future.

Well, that wasn't completely true. I knew we were in trouble if Greg didn't sack up. Now. "I promise."

Greg went paler than usual, then turned back to the faerie girl and pressed his mouth to her neck. He went to one knee as the first fresh blood in a decade splashed against his tongue.

I could smell the blood when he broke the skin, and the smell just about drove me nuts. Imagine your mom's fried chicken, with homemade biscuits, gravy and fresh cherry pie for dessert. Well, this faerie's blood smelled like all of that and more, and I could hardly wait for Greg to top off the tank and pass the entree over.

After a long moment, he finished drinking and just knelt there, leaning over the girl with his forehead on her shoulder. I really hoped I wasn't in for a long talk about feelings and other crap when we got home. Greg stood and waved the girl over to me, turning so he didn't have to watch the feeding.

Not being possessed of Greg's moral fortitude, I took a knee instantly and sank my fangs deep into the girl's carotid. The hot blood flooded my mouth, and I saw stars for a second before I got myself under control. Apparently faerie blood is a lot more nourishing than human blood, because I'd drank barely a pint before I felt completely revitalized.

I stood up, giving the girl a kiss on the forehead that left bloody lip prints just below her hairline, and looked around with new eyes at the great hall. Everything had an extra little sparkle, like the first time a nearsighted kid gets new glasses. I could smell a hint of lavender in the air, and I thought I could taste a hint of it, too. I knew it was coming from Sabrina, and I closed my eyes, listening to her heart beat for a long moment, losing myself in its rhythms before I snapped back to the present. I locked eyes with the Faerie Queen, and she smiled a knowing smile at me.

"Did you enjoy your meal, vampire?" she asked with a tilt of her head.

"She was delicious, Your Majesty." I sketched a brief bow, and the girl returned to her serving duties.

"Excellent. Now the rest of us may dine while we discuss what business has brought a Peacekeeper with two assassins to my lands."

She clapped her hands, and an army of serving girls, all looking eerily identical to the faerie Greg and I had just fed from, came in carrying sections of wood that assembled almost by themselves into a huge banquet table. Once the table was in place, Milandra clapped her hands once more, and a feast appeared in the blink of an eye. Fruits in all colors of the rainbow, vegetables that looked like nothing I'd ever seen before, and a roasted flamingo appeared from nowhere. Literally from nowhere. Milandra clapped her hands, and food just *appeared.*

I sipped a nice red wine while the mortal types ate and Otto recapped the troll fight for the queen. I couldn't process most of what was said because I was still hung up on the word "assassins." Apparently here in Faerieland vampires were not uncommon, and we were used as assassins.

Eventually I raised my hand tentatively, and Milandra nodded towards me. "Um . . ." I hate it when I get tongue-tied, but I was really in uncharted waters here. "Your Majesty, we're not assassins. I mean, we are vampires, that's pretty obvious, but we didn't come here to kill anyone." Which might not have technically been true, but since I didn't know who we might have to kill, I figured that bit might best be left unsaid.

"Then why have you come here, mortal?" Milandra turned to Sabrina, who apparently had been elected general when I wasn't looking.

"We are investigating a series of troll attacks in our world. Otto—um—Octavian led us to believe that you may be able to help us find out where the monsters are coming from, and why they are attacking changelings," Sabrina said, with a glance to Otto, who nodded slightly.

Sabrina went on "My . . . a member of my family has been injured, and Octavian tells us he can only be cured by a plant found here in Faerie. He will die within days if we don't get the plant and get back to him."

Otto stood and bowed to the queen. "Your Majesty, if I may?"

She gave him a negligent wave, and he continued. "The changeling Stephen Neal has been poisoned by the *verdirosa* venom. He seems to have been beaten by a troll wearing *blanthrons.*"

Milandra sat rigidly in her chair, her face a cold mask. "You are telling me that not only has a troll escaped into the mundane world, in the same city where you are supposedly protecting my changelings, but he has now poisoned one of my subjects using forbidden magics? And you were incapable of stopping this and are now paired with a *human* and her pet *leeches?*"

Otto dropped to one knee at the steel in the queen's voice.

I stood up to protest being called a leech, but Sabrina grabbed my wrist. "Sit down," she whispered.

I looked around, and the two guards were a *lot* closer than they had been just a few seconds before.

Otto spoke, his gaze still focused on his toes. "My Lady, I apologize most sincerely for my failure. The slight was mine entirely. I was investigating the attacks, just as I was ordered. The humans simply stumbled upon an attack more recently than I could, given my limited resources."

This seemed to satisfy the pissed-off little faerie girl, at least enough that some of the fire went out of her gaze. She sipped from a goblet and appeared to contemplate the news Otto had delivered.

After a long few seconds of silence, she looked down the table to where Otto knelt. "Rise, Octavian. I am not wroth with you. Be seated." He did as he was told, and Milandra took another drink, then spoke again. "We in House Armelion have no dealings with trolls, but I may be able to summon their master here for a . . . conversation, if that is what you desire."

Something about her tone made the hair on the back of my neck stand up, and looking over at Otto I could tell that there was something going on here that was most definitely not being said. Sabrina didn't catch whatever warning tone I was hearing, and just replied with "Yes, Your Majesty, we would like that very much."

"We may even be able to provide you with the cure you seek for your cousin. The *verdirosa* is a dangerous plant to find, and even more dangerous to harvest. I believe my apothecary keeps one in his garden for just such an occasion as this. If it is here, you may have it. We will not abandon our people who live across the veil."

"Thank you, your Majesty. Thank you very much," Sabrina said, and I could see the tension flow out of her.

"You are most welcome, human. We could no more abandon our changelings than any of our children. But of course, there is a cost."

The knot building in my stomach reached Gordian proportions, and I knew life had just gotten uglier. Again.

"A cost, Majesty?" Sabrina asked.

"Of course, human," Milandra said. "If it is a boon you seek from the Queen of House Armelion, then it is a boon you shall have." She was smiling way too much for me to feel comfortable, and then she dropped the other shoe. "Once you have completed your quest, of course."

I knew it. Outsmarted by another supernatural chick. The last time this happened, I ended up immortal and with weird dietary restrictions. I just hoped we all survived this one.

Chapter 15

I took a deep breath, stood up, brushed off the knee of my jeans and squared my shoulders, looking right at the Faerie Queen. "All right, Your Majesty, what do need us to do?"

I heard Sabrina gasp a little at my directness, but I figured we were down to the real deal now, so any pretense of formality could go out the window.

Milandra chuckled a little and said, "You are wiser than you appear, vampire, not that that takes much. There is a beast that has been plaguing the western border of my lands for some years now. I would like for you to go there, and bring me its heart as proof of your success. Of course, simply returning alive will be proof enough, as none of the other heroes I have sent on this quest have ever been seen again." There was that little half smile again.

I was really starting to want to smack this chick, magical queen or not. She might look like a storybook picture, with her blonde hair and her fluttery silk gown, but there was steel underneath that porcelain skin.

"Okay, Your Majesty. Would you like to enlighten me as to what kind of creature we'll be fighting, or would you rather we be surprised?" I asked

Greg and Sabrina were on their feet now, Greg shaking his head at me, and Sabrina keeping an eye on the guards just in case they didn't approve of my attitude.

"Oh, I wouldn't dream of having you attempt this quest without proper preparations, vampire. After all, dragon-hunting is not for the faint of heart."

I didn't bother mentioning that my heart didn't really beat anymore, faint or not. I was a little hung up on the casual use of the word "dragon."

"Excuse me, Your Majesty?" Greg asked politely. He even raised his hand. "Did you say 'dragon?'" His voice squeaked a little, and now he sounded like he was almost twelve instead of closing in on forty.

"I did indeed, vampire."

"Does 'dragon' maybe have a different meaning here than it does in our world?" he asked, hopefully.

Milandra cocked her head. "In your world does 'dragon' mean a gigantic winged lizard, roughly the size of a barn, with a twenty-foot long poisonous barbed tail, a head the size of a small bedroom with hundreds of razor-sharp teeth, claws the length of broadswords and just as sharp, with breath of fire?"

"Yes, that's pretty close." Greg said in a very small voice. "Except in our world, these are purely mythical creatures. They don't really exist."

I saw a little glimmer of hope in his face until Milandra spoke again. "You mean fantastical creatures of the imagination, like trolls, vampires and faeries?"

"Yes, Your Majesty, just like that." Greg looked about like I felt, which was kinda like I'd been kicked in the guts by a horse. Or a troll.

"Well, then I assure you, Mr. Knightwood, that this dragon is every bit as mythical as you are. But do not despair, my friends, I would not dream of sending you into battle with such a creature garbed in such inadequate clothing."

With that, she clapped her hands, and Greg and I were suddenly wearing suits of bright metal chain mail, complete with breastplates, arm guards and plates over our shins and thighs. Helmets appeared floating in midair in front of us, open-faced things with silver wings sweeping out from the sides. I grabbed mine and put it on, and looked over at Greg.

"I don't want to think about how much metal went into wrapping your gut, bro," I quipped, and then turned to look at Sabrina, and my mouth dropped open.

She looked like an over-sexed Valkyrie, with her own winged helmet, chain mail and breast plate, but where Greg and I had on chain mail leggings, she had an armored skirt that was slit up way higher than I thought was exactly practical. Her breastplate had some obvious concessions to anatomy, with a couple of vents in interesting places showing a little more flesh than I would have expected. All in all, I was pretty distracted by the image, and I figured any enemy might be as well. I was less sure about what effect her appearance would have on a huge lizard, but at least I'd have some eye candy while I was being chomped to death.

"Um, Your Majesty?" Greg raised his hand again. I'm gonna have to teach him to grow a pair one of these days, but I decided that being on our best behavior here probably wasn't a bad idea.

"Yes, vampire?"

That still bugs me. It's like people think it's a title or something. We have names, after all. We don't go around calling people "human."

"This armor is great and all, but we're going to need some weapons, too. Don't you think?" That's when I noticed that my daggers had gone wherever my clothes had, since they weren't on my belt anymore. Just as well, I doubted a six-inch blade would do much against a dragon anyway.

"Of course, Gregory. Follow me. I will take you to my armory." With that, she turned and headed through a door in the side of the room that I was pretty sure hadn't existed before that second. It reminded me yet again how much I hate magic.

We followed Milandra down a long marbled hallway until she stopped in front of a thick wooden door flanked by two knights holding huge polearms. She gestured to the door, and it opened.

With a wave of one regal hand, Milandra said "You may arm yourselves with anything you find within. Choose carefully, as your lives may depend on the decisions you make here."

I went in first, and my heart sank a little as I looked around. Racks and racks of swords, shields and armor filled the huge room, with dozens of bows, crossbows and spears leaning against a far wall. I looked around the whole room a couple of times, then looked back at Greg and said, "Hey Frodo, you see anything in a 9mm around here?"

Greg stopped waving a battle-axe around and said, "Of course not, dude. We're in the realm of the Fae, a world of magic. There's not going to be a gun shop anywhere to be found."

I passed a crossbow over to Sabrina and said "Too bad for you, chica."

She sighted down the length of the crossbow and set it aside, walking to the wall of bows instead. She picked up a short recurved bow and drew it experimentally. "This works for me. Reminds me of summer camp." She picked up a quiver of nasty-looking barbed arrows and said, "I should probably stay out of range as much as possible, not being gifted with super-strength, speed or healing."

"Good idea." I hefted a huge claymore with one hand. It was a little long, but having vampire strength definitely made me able to swing the six-foot sword one-handed, even if I couldn't exactly bring it back around quickly. After a couple of practice swings I put the oversized toothpick away and picked up a shorter, thinner sword that looked like it was designed for one- or two-handed use. "This seems to suit me just fine." For good measure, I dropped a wicked-looking spiked mace in a hip sheath then slid the sword over one shoulder.

Greg strapped on a pair of broadswords, and we were about to head back out into the hallway when something caught the corner of my eye.

"Hey, Sabrina, try this on," I said as I handed her a battered, plain leather sheath with a thin double-edged long sword in it.

Sabrina belted on the scabbard and drew the sword, slashing the air experimentally a couple of times. The blade had a slight reddish sheen to it, and the hilt fit her hand like it was made for her. "This is perfect, Jimmy. Thanks. I hope I don't get close enough to that beast to need it, but if I do, this will be just the thing."

I ducked out into the hall, almost bowling over Milandra, who stood there waiting for me. Greg and Sabrina chuckled a little and went back to arming themselves, picking out a few daggers and things to round out their arsenal.

When they finished in the armory, they joined Milandra and me in the hallway. The queen handed me a glass globe that seemed full of a bluish smoke and said, "I can use my magic to transport you to the forest where the dragon makes his lair. When you have the creature's heart firmly in your grasp, smash this globe on the ground and stand close together. The globe will return you to my great hall. I wish you luck."

Then, with a wave of her hands and a flash of pink and purple faerie dust (yes, really), we were off to slay a dragon.

Chapter 16

Apparently Faerieland dragons live just like you'd expect them to—in caves deep in dark forests. Because that's exactly where Milandra dropped us, right outside a cave in what looked and felt like a deep forest. The ground was carpeted with thick undergrowth, there was moss hanging from the branches and the mouth of a cave gaped hungrily in front of us.

I stood there for a few seconds getting my bearings (or my courage), then took a deep breath and marched resolutely forward . . . only to trip over Sabrina's outstretched leg and fall flat on my face into a plant that I really hoped wasn't poison ivy or something with fingers. I have no idea if I can still get poison ivy since I'm dead, but I wasn't really interested in finding out. I scrambled back to my feet and whirled to face the grinning cop.

"What the hell was that about?" I demanded.

"Do you have a plan, Brainiac?" she asked.

"Yeah. Go in the cave. Kill dragon. Carve out dragon's heart. Go back to the palace. Get the magic plant from Faerie Queen. Eat another faerie chick. Save your cousin. Make trolls stop beating up gay men in my city. Go home. Drink beer. Did I leave out anything important?"

"Maybe how we're going to accomplish the whole 'kill dragon' step," she said, looking around us as if trying to find something. "Look at the mouth of that cave. Can anything as big as Milandra described get through that opening?"

I had to admit that it looked pretty small for anything dragon-sized. The cave opening was about ten feet tall and maybe a little wider than that. Certainly not as big as I would expect for a dragon's lair. "Okay, you've got a point. So what's your plan, General Patton?"

She waved an arm at the forest around us. "We explore the whole area carefully, make sure there isn't another entrance or escape route for the dragon, and then plan our assault."

I hate it when she's right. I hate it even more because she's *always* right.

"Okay," I said. "That does make a lot of sense. Why don't I go this way, you and Greg go that way, and we'll meet back here in about thirty minutes to make a plan."

"Sounds good to me, but why are you going off alone?" she asked.

"It's not that I'm going off alone, but to be brutally honest, I'm not the most graceful thing in the forest, and neither is Greg. If he and I split up, then anything that hears us will wonder why there are two rampaging elephants rummaging in the forest outside a dragon's lair. Hopefully the noise will be so distracting that any beasties will decide to leave us alone instead of attacking."

"Hey!" Greg protested. "I'm stealthy. Like a ninja." He leaned on the trunk of a tree, which proved to be rotten and toppled over, taking my pudgy vampire ninja to the ground in a crash.

"Yeah, you and Kung Fu Panda, bro."

I headed off into the forest as quietly as possible, which really wasn't that quiet. I'm a city vampire, despite spending my college years at Clemson, which is about as rural a college as you can get and still have big-time football. I don't spend a whole lot of time in the great outdoors, mostly because there's never anybody to eat out there. The wilderness is wild, man. I'll stick to places with delivery.

I wandered around for about ten minutes until I came to what looked like the front of the cave. Now *that* looked like something a dragon could get into. The opening was easily fifty feet wide and thirty feet high. The ground in front of the cave mouth was packed hard and smooth, like something really, really big and heavy used this entrance often. I looked up and saw Greg and Sabrina coming around the other side of the hill.

"I guess this is probably the front porch," I said when they reached me.

"Yep," Sabrina said. "Now what do you think about a frontal assault, Braveheart?"

"Might not be my best idea ever," I admitted. "What does your plan smell like, Sun Tzu?"

"Actually, it's Greg's plan." She waved at my partner, who was bringing up the rear as he fought his way through more of those ass-poking thornbushes. I'd never been so grateful for a long hauberk as when I walked through those woods. And yes, I know what a hauberk is. I played D&D.

"Then we're doomed. I'm pretty sure we don't have the cheat codes for this boss fight, gamer-boy," I said as Greg sat down heavily on a boulder.

"Maybe not, but I've still got a pretty good idea for how to make a dragon trap," he panted.

"I'm all ears, bro," I said.

"No, Jimmy, you're usually all mouth. But I'll take it. I saw this in a movie once, so I know it'll work."

My partner's faith in the world of make-believe is eclipsed only by his encyclopedic knowledge of bad movies. He pulled a dagger from his belt and started to sketch out a diagram in the dirt.

"You and I get up to the top of the cave mouth with our swords. Sabrina goes back around to the back door and sneaks in with her bow. She shoots the dragon in the butt with a few of those nasty arrows, and when it comes running out the front door, we jump on its head and kill it. If we each go for an eye, we should be able to stab straight into the brain and drop the beast without any fuss or bloodshed."

"At least on our part," Sabrina said.

"Yeah, shedding a whole lot of dragon blood is sorta the plan," Greg agreed.

I hated to admit it, but it sounded pretty solid, especially the part where Sabrina stayed back and didn't get in the way of the teeth and claws part of the fight.

"What about the whole fire-breathing thing?" I asked. "Won't the dragon just turn around in the cave and roast Sabrina?"

"I'll have to scout it out. Hopefully there'll be a crevice or a crack in the wall I can hide in." She didn't seem too concerned about going into a cave to shoot a dragon in the ass, so I figured, let her go for it. I was the one volunteering to jump off a cliff onto the same dragon's head, after all, so I didn't have a whole lot of room to talk about good decision making.

"All right, boy genius. Do we do this now, or wait 'til dark?" I asked.

"I don't know. I have no idea if dragons are nocturnal or diurnal," Greg replied.

"Since I have no idea what that second thing means, I guess I don't know either," I said. I'm not really an idiot, but Greg is really well-read and likes to show off in front of girls. I do too, but I do most of my showing off by hitting things very hard.

"Diurnal means that a creature is active during the day," said a new voice directly behind me.

I jumped about eight feet in the air and landed eye to very, *very* large eye with the golden-scaled head of a dragon.

Apparently dragons can move very quietly when they want to. I scrambled backward, and out of the corner of my eye saw Greg and Sabrina doing the same thing. I tried hard to stay directly in the monster's field of vision as they moved out to flank the creature's head.

"Good afternoon, heroes. I am Tivernius. Welcome to my forest. I do wish you would put that away, my dear. I would prefer not to incinerate you quite this close to my home. After all, only we can prevent forest fires."

Sabrina put down the bow and the arrow she had been trying to slowly draw, and Greg and I sheathed our swords.

"Thank you. Now please, come into my home and we can continue this conversation in a more civilized setting. I give you my word that I will bring no harm upon you as long as you do not attack me." With that, the head the size of a Mini Cooper pulled back into the cave on a long, scaly neck.

We stood there for a moment looking at each other until finally Sabrina started walking toward the mouth of the cave. "Where are you going?" I almost shouted.

"I'm going to do as he asked," she said. "If he wanted to kill us, we'd already be dead. He caught us completely flat-footed, and let us off the hook. I'm going to give him the courtesy of a conversation before we fight, at least." With that, she leaned her bow and quiver against the cave mouth and followed the head into the side of the hill.

I looked at Greg, who shrugged back at me and followed her. I waited there for just a moment before I realized that they were in no hurry to come to their senses, and followed my friends into the dragon's lair.

Chapter 17

The passage was long and deceptively winding. We walked for a solid five minutes down the tunnels until the passageway opened into a huge room that made Milandra's great hall look like a college dorm. The ceiling vaulted high above our heads, at least fifty feet into the air, and at a glance, I figured you could have fit a couple of football fields in the room with space left over for at least half a racetrack to boot.

Everywhere around us was opulence decked in gold. The floor was made up of marble slabs set in place and lined with gold. The walls were covered in enormous tapestries in amber, gold and orange hues. The ceiling, almost high enough to have its own weather, was sculpted to look like there was a canopy of trees, all covered in golden leaves.

I was almost disappointed not to see a huge lizard lying sprawled on piles of treasure, but there was no huge pile of booty. No fire-breathing monster running its talons through piles of gemstones, no priceless works of art carelessly piled around the room. There was just a sparsely, expensively decorated hall, with a large table near one wall. Seated at the head of the table was a tall, well-built man who rose when we entered and beckoned us to him.

Something about him looked familiar, but I couldn't put my finger on it. He was dressed entirely in shades of gold, with long blonde hair tied back in a ponytail. He wore golden chain mail, which must have weighed a ton, but he stood and moved with the grace of a ballet dancer. A long sword hung at his belt, and judging by the way his biceps bulged under his armor, he knew how to use the thing. At a glance he looked to be in his late twenties, but something in his eyes made him look far older.

"Come, my guests. Sit, be welcome, and I will have food summoned."

We sat at the table, and our host took his chair at the head of the table. "Welcome. Thank you for agreeing to join us. Now, please, what can I do to help you?"

"I'm sorry if I'm missing something, pal, but wasn't there a dragon in here a few minutes ago?" I asked, sipping from a goblet that appeared in front of me, full of rich red wine. The wine had a coppery tang to it, as though there was a little blood mixed in. I wasn't going to complain, but I had my concerns for Sabrina if we were all drinking from the same carafe.

"I am sorry, my friend. I should have realized that you were not from our land. I am Tivernius. I am the dragon."

I looked sharply at the man and could see just a faint hint of scale at his eyebrows. As I looked closer, I saw that the golden tinge to his complexion was more than just a reflection off his armor, he actually had golden skin. I shook my head and reminded myself that we were in Faerieland, after all.

"Sorry. I thought you'd be bigger." When in doubt, quote *Roadhouse*. It's a philosophy that has served me poorly for many years, but I'm too stubborn to change it.

"We have multiple forms, my vampiric friend, just as you do," Tivernius said.

"Huh?" Greg said. "We don't have multiple forms, we're just vampires."

"Then you have been poorly taught indeed, or are very young for your kind, not to have discovered your other shapes," said the dragon-man, a little surprise coloring his voice. "But it is not for me to teach you. Why are you here? Are you also here for my head, like the others that Fae-witch has sent in the past?"

"Well . . ." I looked for a delicate way to put it and couldn't come up with one. "Milandra did send us, but I'm really hoping that we can come to some type of non-violent agreement." Mostly because I couldn't think of a single way that we could fight this guy in dragon form that didn't end up with my femurs being used for toothpicks. I thought we might have a chance at him in human form, but then I looked at his arms again and that sword, and I wasn't so sure.

"And how do you suppose we do that, vampire? She sent you here, didn't she? And she told you that the only way to get her help is to bring back my head? She's been doing this for months, ever since the last time our negotiations broke off."

"Actually," Sabrina interjected, "we're only supposed to bring back your heart. She didn't say anything about your head."

"Well, isn't that just perfect," the dragon-man fumed. "She refuses to marry me. Then she sends bounty hunters and assassins to rip out my heart. Like she hasn't done a good enough job of that herself." He stood up abruptly, toppled his chair over backward and paced back and forth at the head of the table.

We all jumped to our feet, hands on sword hilts, as I fully expected to be flambéed at any moment.

"Well, maybe . . . nah, I got nothing. Sorry," Greg said after thinking for a minute.

"What were you going to say, vampire?" Tivernius picked up his chair and sat back down. He put his elbows on the table and leaned forward, running fingers through his shoulder-length blonde hair. The dude really did have a serious gold-tone thing going on.

"I was just thinking . . . nah, it just doesn't work out." Greg tried to start again, but gave up.

"Spit it out, bloodsucker. I'm sorry, that was uncalled for. I'm just so frustrated by the whole thing that I don't know what to do." He leaned further forward, his chin in his hands. If I didn't know that he could turn into something big enough to swallow bison whole, I would have thought he was just another schmuck with girl troubles. As it was, he was a schmuck that could level entire city blocks with girl troubles.

"Well, why don't you tell us the story? Maybe we can come up with something to help," Sabrina said. "After all, we're here, and we don't really want to try to carve your heart out, and we're in no hurry for you to barbeque us or whatever, so what harm can come from it?"

"That sounds like a fair idea, young human. Have some more wine." He waved a hand and two carafes appeared. The larger red carafe for Greg and me, and another carafe of white for Sabrina.

"Stay outta the red, Sabrina. Just trust me," I said, filling my glass.

She gave me a look, but didn't say anything.

"It all began at a party," Tivernius began. "I attended a ball in the lands of House Cintharion, a neighboring realm to Armelion. The King of Cintharion was ailing, and he wanted me to meet his daughter, in hopes of building an alliance marriage. But she was a harpy with a terrible disposition and a huge nose, and I wasn't interested. I may weigh seven tons and have scales, but I have my standards. She was a truly unattractive human, not in appearance but demeanor, entitled and possessing a ridiculous sense of self-importance. So I was standing at the bar being miserable, because that is where one stands at a party to be miserable, when Milandra walked in."

"Cue harp music," I muttered, earning myself a sharp look from Sabrina but a chuckle from Tivernius.

"Exactly, vampire. The moment I saw her, I was awestruck by her beauty, her carriage and her very *rightness*. Even at her young age I had never seen anyone so suited to rule. She was not yet queen but already the most regal thing in the room. I introduced myself, and we spent the rest of the night talking about everything under the sun and moon. We connected on a deeper level than I have ever connected with any living being, human, faerie, sanguine or dragon."

"I was in love, if you can imagine. Me, who had seen seventeen centuries without ever giving my heart to another creature, completely smitten in one glance. And by a faerie, one of the most capricious races in all the realms. It was inconceivable, but we continued to correspond, and to build a relationship, and we began making plans to marry."

"Wait a second," I interrupted. "You were going to marry Milandra?"

"Yes, of course," answered the dragon. "We were very much in love."

"But she's a faerie. And you're a lot of things, but faerie isn't on the list."

"Don't be speciesist, vampire. It's petty. Any creature of magic can control his or her form, and we can all intermarry if we choose. And what creature is more magical than a faerie, unless it is a dragon? We are magical, we are immortal, and we were in love. Why should we not marry?"

"You're immortal?" I asked.

"Yes. I can be killed, if anyone is brave enough and skilled enough, but I will never die of natural causes. By the way, you're not."

"I'm not what?" I asked.

"Skilled enough. The three of you never had a chance to kill me. That's why you're down here sitting at my table. I'm as safe from you as I am from old age."

Tivernius leaned back in his chair and sipped his wine while I processed all this. "Okay, so you're in love with Milandra, and she's in love with you. And you guys are planning a wedding. And then suddenly something goes wrong."

"All true," he said.

"So what happened? Why aren't you living over there with Milandra in faerie/dragon bliss or whatever?" Greg asked.

"She became queen. I attended her coronation ball, we danced, we laughed, we kissed. It was glorious." The sappy dragon's voice trailed off into blissful memory. I cleared my throat.

"Then within a matter of days, she turned cold. She would not speak to me, would not return my messages, would not receive my visits. Nothing I did would persuade her to allow me back into her presence, even for a moment so that I might understand what offense I have given."

"So, she dumped you?" Sabrina asked.

"Not only that, but it was then that she started sending these so-called heroes to murder me. Month after month, year after year, fools like you come to my home and attack me without warning. I kill them all, but still more come. I grow weary of this. Perhaps I should let you kill me and end my suffering."

"Okay. That makes it a lot easier on us," I said, standing up.

Sabrina put a hand on my wrist as I reached for my sword. "If you touch that sword I swear to God I will stake you in your sleep," she said through gritted teeth.

"Look, I love a good romance as much as the next guy. Which is to say not at all. But anyway, I don't mind the lovey-dovey crap as long as it doesn't get in the way of the important stuff. Like saving your cousin's life. We're on a deadline, remember?"

"I remember. But I don't think he's just going to let us carve his heart out. Besides, something about this doesn't pass the sniff test." She turned back to the dragon, who was weeping very quietly into his wine. "Tivernius, you said that there was a woman whose father wanted you to marry his daughter before you met Milandra?"

"Yes, Alethea of Cintharion. A terrible woman."

"But socially important?" Sabrina continued.

I looked from cop to dragon and back, starting to follow where she was going.

"Yes, she is now sole ruler of the kingdom, as she has yet to find a man willing to marry her."

"So she was at Milandra's coronation as well?"

"Of course."

"Can faeries glamour each other?"

"Sometimes. If they're very powerful. I fail to see what this has to do with anything."

"You would. You're a man. One with scales and a tail the length of a basketball court, but still a man. Look, Tivernius, I've got an idea. It might not work, and if it doesn't, Milandra will probably kill you herself. But if it does, you get to be with the woman you love. So, you willing to try something a little crazy?"

The dragon stood, a little unsteady from all the wine, and all the whining, and glared at Sabrina. She didn't flinch. I guess after you've been to Hell and Faerieland, one bitchy drunken dragon loses the power to intimidate.

"I would do anything to touch her hand but for one instant, human. Do not toy with me. If you make promises that you cannot keep, the consequences will be dire."

I was pretty familiar with my mouth writing checks that my ass couldn't cash, but it wasn't Sabrina's normal *modus operandi*.

"I can promise that if you will accompany us back to the great hall of Armelion, you will be able to be with your love forever, or at least until somebody kills one of you." Sabrina walked back over to the table, took a last swig of wine, grabbed a big napkin and wrapped a couple of loaves of bread in it. Then she soaked the whole bundle with my leftover red. She looked at me and my flabbergasted partner, laughed a little, and said, "On your feet, Greg. We're blowing this pop stand."

She came to stand with me and Tivernius, Greg hot on her heels. "Now," she said, looking at Tivernius. "When we arrive, stay out of sight. I want to announce you my way, and in my time. Okay?"

"I will do as you ask, just bring me into the presence of my lady once more." Tivernius waved a hand, and with a flash and a disconcerting twist of reality, we were back in Milandra's great hall.

I looked around for the dragon, but could only see Sabrina and Greg.

"We have returned, Your Majesty, and we have with us the heart of the dragon!" Sabrina raised the wine-soaked bundle high in the air, dripping a realistic-looking stream of blood onto the marble floor. Milandra stood, looked at the "blood" spilling onto her stonework, and fell to her knees weeping.

Chapter 18

Sabrina didn't hesitate, just looked at me and Greg, whispered, "Don't say a word," and ran to the distraught monarch's side. I stood right where I was, understanding through years of experience that nothing good would come from me interfering with a woman's plan, much less the plan of an armed woman who knew all the ways to kill me.

Sabrina reached the queen and knelt beside her, bag of bread on the floor just out of Milandra's reach. "What's wrong, Your Majesty? I thought you wanted the monster dead? Have we somehow displeased you?"

Greg whispered "Oscar-worthy" in a tone that only I could hear.

Milandra looked up at Sabrina, and in between sobs managed to say, "I loved him, you idiot human! He betrayed me, and broke my heart, but I loved him. I held out hope for a century that he would return to me, even after his dalliance with that Cintharion bitch, and now he's gone." The queen pulled herself together a little and rose, sniffling.

"Your Majesty, I am sorry," Sabrina said. "I had no idea. What happened? You said you loved him?"

"Yes, human. I loved him. Dragons, like your sanguine and the Fae, have many forms, and his human guise was very pleasing to me. He was my heart's mate, and I was willing to give him anything. Until I saw him kissing Alethea of Cintharion at my coronation ball. To betray my love was bad enough, but to betray me in my very throne room, at my coronation . . . well, it was more than I could bear. I sent many valiant warriors to tear out his heart and bring it back to me, hoping perhaps that Tivernius himself would return to me one day. I would have forgiven him, had he but apologized. It took most of a century, but I realized that my love is stronger than my anger."

Sabrina looked back at us and tilted her head to where Tivernius was hiding behind a column. She whispered "keep him hidden" under her breath so that only a vampire could hear, and I nodded at her.

Tears still streamed down her face, but Milandra was one of those women that could cry in public and still be beautiful. And now her beauty was turning cold as her shock changed to anger. The pink marble floors were slowly turning gray, shot through with veins of black and blood-red. I remembered what Otto said about the very stone reflecting Milandra's moods, and started to worry. The little queen was getting seriously pissed off, and if Sabrina's plan didn't work soon, we were going to have to fight a whole dimension just to stay alive.

"But you're the queen. You can do whatever you want. Your whim commands the clouds in the sky, your slightest wish makes the grass turn pink. If you wanted to marry Tivernius, why not tell him?" Sabrina prodded.

"I couldn't!" the queen almost shouted. "He betrayed me. Humiliated me on my own coronation day. I couldn't grovel to him after that. I would be the laughingstock of all the realms. And now I shall be forever alone."

It was getting dark in the throne room, and I didn't feel good about getting out of there, with or without Stephen's cure.

Milandra collapsed again into sobs, and Sabrina motioned for me to bring Tivernius to her.

I'd figured out where Sabrina was going somewhere between the reveal of the dragon's "heart" and the marble turning black. I got almost all the way to the sobbing queen before saying, "What if you were wrong, Your Majesty? What if you were not betrayed, but merely tricked by Cintharion glamour?"

Silence crashed down around us. The temperature in the throne room dropped thirty degrees and frost filled the veins in the marble. Milandra's eyes went wide, then began to narrow in fury as she caught sight of Tivernius for the first time.

"What is the meaning of this, vampire?" Milandra's eyes bored holes in Tivernius.

I needed to talk fast. "You told us that the Fae have multiple forms. And tons of magic, right?"

"Of course."

"And Tivernius told us that Alethea's father wanted him to marry *her*, not you. Right?"

Tivernius spoke, his gaze locked on Milandra's eyes. "Yes. The horrid woman was always pawing at me like I was her property. She even announced our bethrothal after I told her I would rather die than marry her."

"So it wouldn't take much for a faerie to magic themselves to look like Tivernius and be 'caught' kissing Alethea, would it?" Sabrina asked.

"So you didn't—" Milandra asked, stepping closer to the dragon.

"I could never," Tivernius replied.

He held out his arms, and the two of them collided like clichéd movie lovers running through the surf. He actually picked her up and swung around in a circle before putting her down and laying a kiss on the Faerie Queen that curled *my* toes.

I looked up at Sabrina as they broke apart, and I would almost swear that I saw a glint of a tear in her eye. She caught me looking of course, and shot me the finger, completely shattering the mood.

After the Faerie Queen and the dragon had finished making out in the great hall, Milandra turned back to Sabrina and said, "I owe you a great thanks, human. You have done what hundreds of heroes over a century have failed to do. You have brought me the heart of my dragon." She leaned her head against Tivernius' chest, and I swear I heard Greg sniffle from behind me.

"Yes, I thank you for bringing me to my love," Tivernius said. "And now, Milandra . . ." he looked down into her eyes and took both her small hands in his. Tivernius went to one knee on the marble floor, and looking up at Milandra like she was the only woman in the world, said, "Will you be mine? Will you stand by me until the stars fall from the sky? Will you fight with me and beside me? Will you love me no matter how ridiculous and set in my ways I am? Will you allow me to worship you for the goddess of beauty that you are? Milandra, Queen of House Armelion, will you marry me and become Lady Tivernia?"

Milandra looked down at him and said, "I will love you until the flowers no longer bloom. I will stand beside you until the sun refuses to rise. I will kiss you every day that these lips draw breath. I will be your Lady Tivernia, and you shall be King of the Armelion Fae. From this moment forward may our kingdoms be forever joined."

She reached down and took his face in both her hands and kissed him gently. He pulled her down to sit on his knee and began to kiss her more seriously. After a kiss long enough for me to wonder where their air was coming from, they broke apart to a loud cheer. I spun around and saw that out of nowhere a crowd of faeries and humans several thousand strong had filled the great hall, all cheering and waving small flags with pictures of faeries riding dragons on them.

I don't care how long I live, I'll never get used to magic.

Chapter 19

We toasted the happy couple, listened to the cheering of the crowd, and generally fidgeted around for an hour or so before I finally pulled Otto aside. "Look buddy, I'm all for marital bliss and immortal happiness, but we've kinda got a guy dying back on the other side of the magic portal, remember?"

"Fear not, James. Our queen has sent for the apothecary, who is on his way to you now with the *verdirosa* plant. Once I have it, we can deal with the Unseelie and return to your world to heal your friend."

"That's great, Otto," Sabrina said from beside me. "What's an Unseelie, and when will they get here?"

Milandra joined us then, waving an arm and sending the reveling faeries to who-knows-where. "The Unseelie are sometimes considered the Dark Fae. They are cousins to the faeries you know, but their magic is practiced not to create, but to destroy. They use their martial abilities to enslave, not to protect. They do not typically discuss, preferring to fight. In short, they are the antithesis of everything we strive to be. They keep trolls as bodyguards and servants, while we destroy the loathsome creatures on sight. If there are trolls making their way into the mundane realms, no doubt the Unseelie will know about it."

Apparently the Unseelie were a bit of an unpleasant topic among the Armelion Fae, like *that* uncle at every Southern family reunion.

"As usual, *your highness*, you prove your ignorance with every syllable." An oily voice came from behind me, and I whirled to see a seven-foot tall faerie standing far too close for comfort. Clad all in black, his white hair made a sharp contrast to his ensemble, and his dark eyes scanned the room for threats like a tiger in a cage. He was just as handsome as every faerie I'd seen so far, but his was a cruel kind of handsome, like the chisel-jawed bad guy from every 80s movie.

He carried two long swords with hilts showing signs of use, and a dagger protruded from the top of each knee-high boot. I thought I saw a couple of small blades tucked into his gloves as well, but I couldn't be sure. What I could be sure of was that this dude was bad news, and that he'd somehow gotten close enough to stab me in the back without me ever hearing him enter the room. I pretty much hated him on sight, and by the look he gave me I'd say the feeling was mutual.

"Count Darkoni, you are welcome to my hall and my lands. I pledge you and yours safe passage and lodging as long as you reside here and maintain the peace with my people and other guests." Milandra crossed the room to stand stiffly in front of her throne, hand on the hilt of a sword I'd never seen before. The hilt was plain silver, with a large sapphire set into the pommel, and the scabbard showed signs of plenty of use.

"Fear not, little queen. We shall behave ourselves while we are here. And if we do not, I have no doubt you will enjoy feeding us to your husband. Or is that why I'm here? Do you tire of your pet lizard already? Or did you bring me here to offer me some consolation prize?" He looked Sabrina up and down like a piece of meat, and licked his lips.

She met his eyes without a hint of fear and walked over to the faerie like she was the queen, not Milandra. She reached up and grabbed Darkoni's collar, pulling him down until they were on eye level.

Very slowly she spoke directly into the faerie's face. "Not if you were the last almost-human left in all the worlds. You couldn't handle me, and you certainly don't deserve me." Then she slapped him across the face with a sound like a .22 going off.

Darkoni's hand flashed out, but I was there first. I caught him by the wrist before he could hit Sabrina, and I gave his wrist a good squeeze. When I could hear the bones grind together, I stopped. Darkoni never flinched.

"Don't even think about touching her, Tinkerbelle," I said through gritted teeth.

"Or what? You'll bleed all over me? Thorgun, show our fanged friend here your hand."

The sleazy faerie smiled down at me as I felt the presence of something very large behind me, and a hand very gently covered my head. My whole head, from crown to jaw, fit inside the huge, smelly troll hand that descended from above me. Thorgun didn't speak or even put any pressure on my scalp, he just rested his hand on my head, holding it like I could palm a baseball. I got it. He could squash my head like a grape before I could even think about hurting his boss. I hate melodramatic monsters.

"Now, why don't we all sit down and behave like civilized beings. Even those of us who obviously are not," Darkoni said.

The hand disappeared from my head. I turned around and looked up, way up at his troll bodyguard. He had nothing on Tivernius' dragon size, but at nine and a half feet tall with fingers as big around as my wrists, I didn't want to arm-wrestle him anytime soon. I let go of Darkoni's wrist, after giving it one last squeeze for good measure. Petty, I know, but sometimes that's how I roll.

"What a lovely idea, Count Darkoni," Milandra said, as though nothing out of the ordinary had happened.

She waved her hands and a table appeared with chairs sized for all the occupants, even Thorgun and his twin, who stood on the other side of Darkoni. The Unseelie count had brought a retinue of about half a dozen faeries with him, but the trolls were the real muscle. Both of them made the one we fought outside the bar look like a half-grown kid, and they had hammers hanging over their shoulders with heads bigger than a dishwasher. We took our seats, our team on one side, the Unseelie entourage on the other side, and Milandra got right down to business.

"Count Darkoni, we have called you here to inquire why there have been troll attacks on changelings in the mundane world. Would you care to enlighten us?" the Faerie Queen asked.

When I glanced at her I saw that she had magically changed into her robes of state and crown. Tivernius was decked out, too, and a golden circlet rested on his head to match the silver one on Milandra's brow.

"I would love to, Your Majesty, if I had any inkling of what you are talking about." The Unseelie count had transformed his wardrobe as well, now garbing himself in robes of deepest black velvet with black fur trim. A black circlet capped his brow, with a large red stone in the center. The stone pulsed rhythmically, almost as if it were in time to a heartbeat somewhere. I looked down to see if my clothes were any different, but it was the same armor I'd put on when I crawled out of bed in the morning.

Oh well, can't have everything.

"Please, Your Excellence, do not play ignorant with us. Your kind has long held enmity for the changelings, and you have much truck with the trolls. If you are not behind these attacks, then who?" Milandra seemed almost to be enjoying the jousting with the snotty faerie, but I wasn't sure she was going to get anywhere.

"Of course we loathe the changelings, but it is the human vermin that we would exterminate, not the innocent Fae that *you* cast out like so much unwanted livestock. We are the rightful lords of this realm, and bringing humans here to breed with and create abominations like yourself is an affront to our true heritage."

I took a closer look at Milandra, and for the first time could see that her ears were a little more rounded than the rest of the faeries I'd seen. Must have been a human branch on her family tree somewhere in the past.

"If we wanted to attack anyone, you would be a more likely target than any poor changelings you've cast away into the mundane world like so much rubbish." Darkoni smiled and leaned back in his chair. "I suppose if that is all you have to ask, then we will accept payment for our travels and leave." He reached for a small bag lying on the table beside Milandra's hand, and she clasped her hand over his wrist before he could withdraw.

The Unseelie stood and drew a knife, pointing the tip at Milandra's wrist. "I suggest you release my arm, before you lose your own, Your Majesty."

I whispered from behind him, "I don't think that's a good idea, Excellence."

He turned his head slightly and saw the point of my dagger hovering right beside his eye. Otto and Greg had the trolls covered, and Armelion knights surrounded the rest of Darkoni's entourage.

"This is an outrage, Milandra," Darkoni shouted, veins bulging in his neck. "We have come here in good faith, answered your questions, and now I wish to take my payment and leave. You stretch the boundaries of hospitality to the breaking point, lizard-slut."

"That's it, I'm drinking him." I grabbed his collar and pulled the count's neck around toward my mouth, only to have him twist in my grasp and stab me in the chest with the dagger he'd threatened Milandra with only seconds before. I looked down at the hilt sticking out of my chest, and then I got really mad. Apparently chain mail is only useful against swords and slashing weapons, because the faerie's dagger went through my armor like a hot knife through butter.

"I really, really liked this shirt, you prick," I said, just before I took him by the neck and one wrist and flung Darkoni across the great hall. He crashed into the far wall and slid down like the coyote in a Saturday morning cartoon. I pulled the dagger out of my chest, looked over at Milandra, and said, "Sorry, but he was a real asshole."

"He's also not dead, bro," Greg said from right beside me. I followed his gaze and saw a very angry Unseelie count heading my way with a sword in one hand and a wicked barbed dagger in the other.

"Crap. Sabrina, cover the queen," I yelled as I reached across the table and grabbed Milandra's sword. "Sorry, Majesty, but you need to not be here for this part. Greg, you with me?"

"Right here." My partner, being the smart one of the pair, had not left his sword in his bedroom this morning. Me, being the good-looking one, would be using a sword borrowed from the Faerie Queen in tonight's entertainment. Then with a howl of rage from Darkoni, the great hall erupted in mayhem and bloodshed.

Chapter 20

Greg and I hopped onto the table to get a better view of things, and I ended up eye-to-eye with Thorgun, who was bringing his giant hammer around for a swing at Otto. I waited until he got the hammer up to the top of his swing to slide my sword into the unprotected space under his arm. A gout of greenish-black blood spurted from the wound, and the troll's eyes rolled back in his head. He started to topple forward, right onto Greg and me.

"Split!" I yelled as he fell forward, and the gigantic body came crashing down, tearing the sword from my grasp and turning the heavy wooden table into toothpicks. Greg and I dove in opposite directions, him landing on the back of an Unseelie man-at-arms with an unpleasant crunching sound, while I went headfirst onto the floor.

I'd love to say I rolled to my feet in a smooth motion and came up with a knife in each hand, but the reality of it is that I sprawled on the marble floor like a skinny fish out of water and lay there for a minute cursing about how bad my knee hurt. After a couple seconds' worth of creative profanity, I stood up and looked around for an abandoned weapon. Thorgun's hammer was lying on the ground, but even with my vamp-strength I couldn't swing that behemoth effectively. I snatched up a shattered board and brought it up just in time to block a sword blow from a very angry Count Darkoni, who smiled as he circled me with his sword and dagger.

"I will enjoy bathing in your blood, vampire," he sneered as I tried to parry all his thrusts.

"Well, since I borrow it, you won't technically be bathing in *my* blood," I said as I took a swing at his head. He ducked easily, and I got a slash across the ribs that my armor turned aside. At least my chain mail was good for something.

"No matter, bloodsucker, it won't be inside you any longer, that's all that matters to me." He lunged with the sword, and I batted it aside easily.

Unfortunately I forgot about the knife in his other hand. At least, I forgot about it until he buried it in my thigh. The barbed blade ripped all sorts of useful things when he jerked it out of me, and I screamed as I fell to one knee.

"Now die, fool," he snarled.

I looked up as he raised his sword for one final thrust, and did the only thing I could think of. I bit him on the inside of the thigh.

Darkoni threw his head back and screamed, then stabbed downward with his sword. My armor deflected the worst of the blow, and he dropped the knife to try a second time with both hands. That cost him valuable seconds, though, and as he raised his blade for another thrust I drained more of his lifeblood with every heartbeat. He summoned up all his remaining strength for another downward cut, and I reached out with my left hand and broke his kneecap, knocking him backward and dislodging me from his leg. Arterial blood spurted high into the air, and I crawled up the count's twitching body to get to his throat.

I stopped right before I bit into him again, and looked him in the eyes. "Now who's sending the trolls?"

The count laughed, a wet, dying sound, and spat in my face. "We have no need to kill our own kind, fool. We wish to purge all the realms of inferior beings, like yourself."

"Well, today's purge isn't going so well for you, asshole." With that, I bit deep into his neck and drew the last drops of blood from his body.

I stood up, faerie blood and battle fury roaring in my veins, and took the count's sword from his dead fingers. I quickly cut off his head, just in case faeries could come back as vampires, and looked around at the rest of the fight.

Sabrina had Milandra backed into a corner behind her and was holding off a pair of Unseelie soldiers who looked like they had bad intentions for the Faerie Queen. Tivernius and Otto were duking it out with Thorgun's evil twin, and they seemed to be holding their own. Greg was swashbuckling with two dark faeries, and the knights seemed to have everything else under control. I tossed Darkoni's sword across the room and through the back of one of the soldiers threatening the queen. His partner turned to watch him fall, and Sabrina cut his head half off with her sword.

I ran to pull Milandra's sword out of Thorgun's armpit, and looked around for something else to punch. I froze as a hand wrapped around my ankle, then yanked up abruptly, upending me onto the floor with a crash of chain mail, plates and vampire parts. I rolled over and looked up, trying to see what was after me now.

I lay there, mouth open as I watched Count Darkoni's body reach down, pick up his head, and jam it back onto his shoulders. The count rolled his shoulders like a boxer loosening up before a round, then picked me up and hurled me across the great hall.

I crashed into a wall and slid ten feet to the floor, still staring at the undead Unseelie. The zombie Count didn't seem any the worse for wear from his recent demise, and he stalked across the room towards Milandra with murder in his eyes. I scrambled to my feet, still high on faerie blood, and blocked his path to the Faerie Queen.

"Just out of curiosity, how many times will I have to kill you?" I asked.

Darkoni just grinned and punched me in the chest. I staggered back several steps and looked down at my dented breastplate. The chest was caved in to a point that breathing was nigh-impossible, and I was pretty sure he'd cracked my sternum. I could *feel* the bones knit as the magical blood in my veins kept me going, and I didn't need to breathe except to talk, so I rushed back at the Count.

His eyes widened at my assault, and I noticed for the first time that his eyes had gone completely black. No pupil, no iris, no nothing. Just black. For some reason, that was creepier than the whole screwing his head back on thing. Probably because dead guys walking around had long since lost their ability to impress me.

But he locked those black eyes on me, raised a hand palm-out in my direction, and I froze. It was like invisible bonds wrapped every inch of me, and I couldn't move a muscle. My eyes widened as the dead faerie closed on me, and it smiled at the terror in my eyes.

The Unseelie faerie stretched a hand out to me, and its fingers glowed with a dark aura, almost like it was surrounded by a halo of blackness, if that's even possible. When it pressed a finger to my forehead, the temperature plummeted and everything went away.

I was suddenly alone, floating in a featureless void with no indication of where I was, *what* I was or what was happening. I thought my eyes were open, but the darkness was so complete I couldn't be sure. A voice came from inside me and all around me, a sibilant whisper that penetrated my skull and ran through my brain like rivers of ice.

The voice latched onto my fear, and spun it into a hurricane.

"You're alone, Jimmy, in a pit as black as your name, as black as your heart. No one can find you here, because no one cares enough to look. You're just another parasite, Jimmy, just another leech to be burned off and thrown aside to shrivel and cook in the sun. You're nothing, less than nothing, because at least nothing can survive on its own. You can't even do that, you worthless bloodsucker."

"You're the lowest of the low, Jimmy. You killed your best friend and made him a monster. You watch your only other friend age and waste away, and now you want to spread your filth to that girl? Why would she want a nothing like you? She can have a real man. A man that she can grow old with. A man she can go out in the daytime with. A man who won't try to kill her while she sleeps and turn her into a soulless abomination. You're nothing. You've always been nothing, all the way back to high school."

"But I can make you *something*, Jimmy. I can make you special. I can make you live again. I can make you whole. I can make you into something she can love. Something she can touch. Something she won't be afraid of. Just say yes, Jimmy. Just let me in, and I"ll make you a real boy."

The voice wrapped around my head and my heart, poking at all my soft spots. I didn't know what it wanted, then I did. Then I knew.

I spoke. "Come here," I whispered.

I could feel it, the *presence* that had been riding along with Count Darkoni. The nasty hitchhiker that wanted to piggyback on my soul for a little while.

"I'm here, Jimmy. Are you ready?"

"I'm ready," I whispered back.

"Say the word, and I'll make you magic."

"Here's a couple of words. Go. Fuck. Yourself." I opened my eyes and I was back in the great hall, half a second after the dead faerie had mojo'd me. I stepped forward, Milandra's sword flashing across the distance between us, and I sliced the count's head cleanly from his shoulders again.

This time, instead of a simple collapse, a black mass rose out of the body with a shriek, spinning faster and faster in a whirlwind toward the high vaulted ceiling, finally disappearing with a flash of crimson light. The body itself crumpled to the floor and dissolved into a steaming pile of dust.

I looked around at where my friends and Milandra's people seemed to have the battle well in hand, and took the opportunity to crawl under the huge table and pass out.

I woke to Greg's toe prodding me in my ribs, none too gently I might add. I looked up at him and felt an indescribable warmth flood through me. I scrambled to my feet and pulled him to me in a tight hug. It wasn't even one of the one-armed bro-hugs that we usually do, it was a full-on hug with my arms wrapped all the way around his pudgy body.

"Thank God you're still alive," I said.

Greg patted me on the back awkwardly and slithered out of my grasp. "Yeah, you too, pal. Really. Glad you're not deader. Now . . . uh, let's just . . . not hug anymore, okay?"

"Yeah, fine. Okay. No more hugging." I looked around, and Sabrina, Milandra, Otto and Tivernius were all looking at me strangely. They kept their distance, as though I might have come down with some kind of weird disease that's spread by hugging.

I held Milandra's sword out to her, hilt-first. "I think this is yours, Your Majesty. Sorry about kinda stealing it."

She held up a hand, then unfastened her sword belt and passed that over to me. "I think you may need it more than I do, James. Especially if what I suspect happened near the end of the battle is true."

"Yeah, dude," Greg said, "what happened to you? I finished off my guys, then helped Otto and Ty take out the last troll, and when we turned around you were out like a light under the table."

"Didn't you see what happened with the Count?" I asked. Greg shook his head, and I looked around at the rest of them.

"I believe I understand what you saw, but I would like to hear you describe everything in your own words," Milandra said.

She waved a hand, and comfortable chairs and drinks appeared. I had to admit, I might not love magic, but I could get used to some of the perks.

I described everything that happened from the time I killed the Count to the time I killed him again, then told them all about the black cloud thing, the void and the whispers. I didn't mention exactly *what* the voice was whispering, preferring to get out of the encounter with a sliver of dignity.

"So, Your Majesty. What was that thing, and how did I run it off?" I asked when I was finished.

"*Sluagh,*" she said, and Tivernius' eyes went wide.

"Bless you," I said. Nobody laughed. "Okay, fine. What's a *sluagh?*"

Milandra actually shivered at the word. "The *sluagh* are souls. In a vast oversimplification, they are the vilest souls to ever walk the earth. Far too foul for Heaven, these creatures are rejected by all the Hells as incapable of redemption. They can touch all realms, but are of none. They wander between the worlds wreaking havoc as they see fit. They can only be slain by weapons of powerful magic, that's why when you slew Darkoni with his sword, the *sluagh* inside him was able to continue manipulating his body as it searched for another host."

"Another host?" I asked.

"You damaged the host body, James. It needed to find another one to inhabit. But it can only bond with a willing inhabitant. When you rejected it, the spirit needed to find another host. Then you struck it with my sword, and that was enough to kill both host and spirit."

"You're telling me your sword is magical, and that I just killed a spirit-creature that's too evil for Hell?" I asked.

"In a nutshell, yes," Milandra replied.

"Shit." I trend toward the profane when truly shocked. "But if I killed it, why do you want me to keep your sword?"

"I have a feeling you're going to need it more than I will. After all, if there was a *sluagh* controlling a pack of trolls here in Faerie, perhaps there is another one commanding the beasts in your realm. If nothing else, think of it as a gift from a grateful wedded couple, with no obligations."

"Thanks, Your Majesty. I'll try not to kill anything inappropriate with it," I said.

"I hate to be the one to break up the party, but can we get home soon? I do still have a cousin dying there," Sabrina said.

"Of course, my dear. Otto will travel with you to administer the cure. He knows how to properly prepare the *verdirosa* so as not to kill anyone who touches it."

"Well that's handy," I said.

Milandra stood and waved her hands in a big circle. A shimmering circle appeared in the hall, and Sabrina stepped through it. Greg followed, and I started toward it.

Milandra held up a hand. "Be careful, James. I feel there may be something larger at work here. In all my years I have never heard of a *sluagh* attacking Faerie. If someone is commanding these creatures, they may be more powerful than we can comprehend."

"Yeah, I'm out of my league. I know. Again," I said as I stepped through the portal.

Chapter 21

We stepped through a glowing golden portal and were suddenly back in my less-than-glowing apartment. No more pink sky, no more Technicolor foliage, just some stains of indeterminate origin on the carpet and a couple of discarded *Magic: The Gathering* card wrappers under the coffee table. Sabrina took one look around, then grabbed her cell phone. I don't have any idea where she hid it under the fanboy's wet dream of armor she wore, but she pulled out the device and breathed a sigh of relief.

"Okay, it seems like it's the same day we left, and according to this . . . that can't be right." She shook the phone, then stared at the entertainment center for a minute, then opened up my laptop and looked at the screen.

"You want to tell me what you're doing, or should I just ask for the warrant, Detective?" I asked, closing the lid on my laptop. I had no recollection of the last thing I'd been surfing, but I was pretty sure it was nothing that I wanted Sabrina to see.

"According to my watch, we've only been gone four hours," she replied.

"Time moves differently in Faerie, Detective. And Her Majesty is the ultimate ruler of the land. She created this portal to bring us back very shortly after we left, so I would have plenty of time to deliver the cure to your cousin."

I turned, and there was a giant bald faerie in my den. Again.

"Hi, Otto. Want a beer?" I asked, heading for the fridge.

"No thank you, James. I would like to deliver the *verdirosa* plant as quickly as possible. It decays rapidly and begins to lose effectiveness soon after it leaves Faerie."

"Then we should roll. I'll drive." Sabrina headed up the stairs grabbing her car keys off the bar as she passed. I didn't move, enjoying the thought that she had a place where she always put her keys in my place, and wondering how far up the stairs she'd get before she realized she was still dressed like She-Ra.

She made it almost to the top, then her chain mail skirt got tangled in her feet, and she turned around. "Would you have let me get to the car in this outfit?" she asked me.

"The car? Oh, yeah. But I would have stopped you before you pulled out onto the street." I went to my bedroom, deposited Milandra's sword in a corner, threw on some clothes that didn't look like they came out of *Lord of the Rings Part IV*, and brought out some sweats and a T-shirt for Sabrina. She went into my room to change, and two minutes later we were ready. Otto, of course, just waved his hands and was dressed like a normal, if slightly more fashionable than usual, Charlottean.

Ten minutes later we were all headed for the hospital. Sabrina led the way in her car, lights flashing as she ran red lights and weaved through traffic with abandon. I tucked right onto her back bumper and enjoyed watching Greg hyperventilate in the passenger seat. For a dude with a muscle car, he panicked at the least bit of NASCAR influence on my driving.

"You know the magical plant is in the car ahead of us, right?" he said through gritted teeth.

"Yeah, so?"

"So why are you driving like a bat out of hell?"

"No puns, etc. etc. Because it's 6:45, dude. And I'd like to be inside the hospital before sunrise."

"Sonofabitch," my partner muttered. "Are we gonna have to hang out in the waiting room all day again?"

"I think we can get somebody to drive us home in the trunk if we need to. Hey, maybe we'll get lucky and it'll snow," I said without much hope. Charlotte, NC, has never been known for its snowfall, even in January. But we might luck out and get a really crappy, rainy, overcast day, and then we'd only get nasty sunburn, not charcoal briquet level sunburn.

We pulled into the hospital parking lot, and Sabrina threw a CMPD placard on her dash. I reached across Greg to pop the glove box, and pulled out a small 'Clergy' placard and placed it on the dash of my car.

"Where did you get that?" Greg asked, his eyes wide.

"Stole it from Mike. Come on." I opened the door and got out.

"I am not misusing a clergy sign to get a better parking place. That's so wrong it's out of bounds even for you," Greg said, getting out of the car and slamming his own door.

"Dude, we eat people. We're not friggin' pantheons of morality, okay. Remember, *vampires*. Nosferatu, Lestat, Dracula, the scary one, not like the goofy dude in that episode of *Buffy*."

"But we're not like that. And I don't eat people."

"Tell that to the faerie chick you nibbled on yesterday."

As soon as I said it, I wanted the words back. Greg's head snapped back like I'd slapped him, and I felt like the world's biggest asshole.

After a second or two of cold silence, I said "Look, man, I'm sorry. I didn't mean anything by it. I know that shit was really hard for you, and I hate that you had to do it. But you had to, and you did, and now it's over."

"It's not over. I can still taste her. And I can smell the blood from every human in a hundred yards. And it smells *good*. I don't know how you think you can control it, but you can't. I can't." He didn't look at me for a long few seconds, and when he did, I stepped back a little from the look in his eyes.

"You go ahead, Jimmy. I'll park the car and meet you up there."

"You sure? I'll go with you to park—"

"Go." The word came from somewhere deep inside him, and I remembered the last time I'd heard Greg sound like that. He had been kneeling over the body of a teenage girl, her throat ripped out and her life's blood staining the front of his T-shirt. I'd almost lost him that night to the animal that lives inside of us, and I didn't know if I could pull him back from the edge again.

After a long moment, I tossed him the keys. "Don't scratch the paint."

That worked. He laughed, and the monster was buried again. Greg, the real Greg, gave me the finger and said "I couldn't find a new place to dent this heap of crap if I tried."

While Greg parked the car, I headed up to see Stephen. Sabrina was standing in the sterile hallway outside his room with Mike. Mike took one look at me and burst out laughing. I glanced over at Sabrina, who was trying hard to restrain herself from doing the same thing.

"What? Did I put my shirt on backward again?" I checked my fly, and Jimmy Jr. was safely tucked away. Then I got a good look at my arm. "No," I whispered, the mere thought of this horror chilling me to the bone. I turned and ran down the hall past the elevators and the waiting area to the public restrooms.

I flung open the door and skidded to a halt in front of the wall of mirrors. Fortunately for me, the hospital went cheap on their mirrors and didn't use real silver backing. Vampires don't reflect in those since the silver screws with our magic. But cheap mirrors, no problem. So I could see exactly what had my friends in hysterics. I was *sparkling*.

Not only was I sparkling, but I was sparkling in colors. Milandra obviously had a sense of humor, since she returned me to the real world with a shower of pink and purple sparkles trailing from my hair. I looked like I'd run naked through a gay glitter factory. I turned on the water and started frantically pulling paper towels from the dispenser and scrubbing myself, but the sparkles were stuck to me with some kind of magic. I was just going to have to look like a cross-dressing stripper, or a teenaged girl's makeup set exploded all over me, until it wore off.

I trudged back to where Mike and Sabrina stood. I stopped in the hallway and did my best runway turn for them. "I sparkle. I get it. It's funny. Pretty soon I'll get angsty and use more hair product. But for now, how's Stephen?"

Mike spoke up. "Your faerie friend is in there with him now. He refused to allow us into the room as he administered his treatment, saying that it could be dangerous to humans. To his credit, Mr. Neal's partner refused to leave. Mr. Glindare made it very clear that he would not be leaving his partner's side for any reason."

"Husband," I corrected.

"You'll have to forgive me if I stick with 'partner,' James. I'm as progressive as I can be, within the limits of Church doctrine. And until the Church recognizes their union, I'm afraid 'partner' is as far as I can go."

I decided not to get in a conversation about separation of church and state with one of my oldest friends in the middle of the lemon-scented hallway of a hospital, so I let it go. Otto came out of the room then, and the scent of the *verdirosa* followed him in a cloud, mixed with something new, something sweeter and a little hint of faerie blood. Otto looked more tired than he had after our fight with the Unseelie, but he smiled as he looked at Sabrina.

"He will heal," Otto said.

Sabrina sagged against me in relief. I wrapped my arms around her instinctively, then tightened them a little when I realized what we'd done. She pulled back, wiping her eyes with the heel of her hand and giving one of those embarrassed little chuckles that people do when they let you see more than they wanted to. But I heard her heart beat, and I heard it speed up a little when I pulled her close, and the sound made me warm, even though the January chill still lingered on my skin.

"Thanks, Otto. That's awesome. Is he awake? Can we go in?" I asked.

Otto waved us on, then turned to leave.

Sabrina stopped him. "Thank you. Really. If you ever need anything, I owe you one."

Otto smiled down at her. "You owe no debt to me, Defender. I did as my queen ordered, and gladly. I provided aid to one of my own, and in doing so brought succor to a friend of my House. But should I require your assistance in the future, I shall call."

"Do that, Otto. We'll be there," I said, holding out my hand.

He smiled, shook my hand, then Sabrina's, then stepped through a glowing portal and vanished.

"I will never get used to that," I said, turning to Stephen's door.

"Wait," Sabrina said. There was a tentative quiver in her voice, completely out of character with the woman who was willing to shoot a dragon in the ass for her cousin. But I guess family can get you where monsters can't touch.

"It'll be fine," I whispered to her. "He still loves you, or he wouldn't have told his husband about you."

She looked at me nervously, then nodded once and put her hand on the door.

"Come on in, cuz. I know you're standing out there getting all worked up for nothing. And bring your pet vampire in, too."

Stephen's voice sounded strong, but if he called me a pet again I might see what I could do about that.

We walked in and Sabrina's cousin was sitting up in bed, looking very little like someone who'd been beaten nearly to death less than forty-eight hours earlier. Mike followed us in, nodding pleasantly to a very confused-looking Alex.

"Ummm, Stephen, did you just call him a . . . ?" Alex trailed off as he looked over at me, seeing nothing about me that screamed "vampire." After all, the traditional mythology does not include skinny, six foot four inch vampires with pointy noses and brown hair that shoots out in every direction out from under a purple Clemson Tigers baseball cap.

I nodded to him, and held out my hand. "Mr. Glindare, good to see you again. I suppose you must be Stephen."

We shook hands, and he looked past me to Sabrina. She stood in the doorway, showing nerves you wouldn't expect from a woman who's traveled to Hell and back for a case, literally.

"You two want a moment alone? A pair of boxing gloves? Dr. Phil?" I asked.

Stephen struggled to a more upright position and held out his arms. Sabrina rushed into his embrace, and you could almost watch a decade of distance vanish in an instant.

"This would be when I say something like 'don't worry, they're cousins,'" I said to Alex.

"Funny, I was thinking I should say the same thing to you." He grinned up at me.

I looked around for a chair. Finding none, I sat on the edge of the bed at Stephen's feet. "Now," I began, "I hate to break up the touching reunion scene, but I'd like to make sure that there's not another one of these things coming back to finish the job. You know it was a troll that attacked you, right?"

"Actually, I had no idea what it was. I was walking to meet Alex after rehearsal, and something grabbed me and pulled me into the alley. It muttered something about me being the next contestant, or something like that, and to come along quietly."

He took a deep breath, and Alex reached over and patted his leg. "It's okay, babe. Take your time."

Stephen continued. "I grabbed my cell phone to call Alex, and the thing just swatted it out of my hand. It punched me in the face, and knocked me cold. The next thing I knew I woke up in a locker room, wearing a pair of shorts and nothing else. Another . . . troll, I guess, was in the room with me, and he shook my hand and told me he was about to kill me. I told him I didn't want any trouble, and he said it was nothing personal, that's just how the fight was scheduled—to the death. Then a door opened, and he walked out of the room. There were all these people out there, and they were all cheering, and screaming for him, and for me."

Stephen looked around, then went on. "Then the door opened again, and two other trolls came in. They dragged me out into this cage, put a sword in my hand, and told me to fight. I threw the sword down, and they put it back in my hand. They told me I could either fight and die, or just die. They left, and the first troll came after me. He had on these huge metal gloves with spikes on them, and I—" He took a sip of water, trying to pull himself together.

"I couldn't do anything against him. I've taken some judo and tae kwon do classes, but this guy was huge, and fast, and I'd been knocked out. He beat the hell out of me. The last thing I remember is him catching me with an uppercut and hearing my jaw crack. After that, it was all black. Then I woke up here, with a bald faerie feeding me magical guacamole."

"Yeah, about that . . ." Alex said, looking from me, to Sabrina, to his husband. I held up both hands and stood, not wanting to get involved in family drama.

Stephen blushed. "Yeah, so . . . Honey, I'm a faerie! That's a lot easier to say when you've been called one your whole life. I'm sorry I didn't tell you, Alex. I just found out about this a couple weeks ago. Up until then I just thought I was, you know, talented."

"Being one of the Fae has nothing to do with your ability at dance, Stephen, just like the fact that I'm a vampire has nothing to do with my rapier-like wit." I paused to glare at Mike, who was suddenly afflicted with a coughing fit. "It just means you're a bit faster, more agile and stronger than a human. And it means you'll probably live forever. Unless that only counts in Faerieland. Then forget I said anything." I threw that last bit in because his husband was right there, and I didn't want to have to watch while they sorted through the whole immortality thing.

"So now where are we?" Sabrina asked. "Instead of a series of random beatings, we've got some kind of underground fight club going on with trolls and faeries, and no idea where to find out more about it."

"Oh, I think I've got a pretty good idea," I said, heading toward the door. "I've got something I want to look into. Sabrina, can you stay here and play catch-up with your cousin for a while? I want to make sure somebody is here in case someone, or something, tries to get at him again. Can you meet us at our place with the case files on all the attacks tomorrow night? I want to look at all the data and start to re-interview the other victims. Maybe one of them remembers something."

"I can do you one better," she said, reaching into her purse and pulling out a USB memory stick. "I've got all of the case files with me, so you guys can start tonight while I hang here with my cousin."

I took the memory stick and tucked it away in my pocket.

"That's great. Mike, can you get in touch with your witch friend and see what she knows about trolls and faeries? Maybe there's some kind of secret Wiccan database that she can tap into. I'll get Greg and we'll look into my lead. Stephen, if you think of anything, give us a call. Sabrina, if anything bad happens, call me immediately. Please do not try to stop a troll on your own." I started out the door and stopped when I realized everybody was still staring at me.

"What?" I asked.

"I think we're all waiting for you clap your hands and yell 'Break!' coach," Sabrina said with a smirk.

"Oh, shut up. And be careful," I said on my way out the door.

"Aye, Aye, Cap'n," Sabrina said to my back as I headed down the hall. "Oh, and one other thing," she yelled. "Take a shower, you sparkle!"

Chapter 22

I caught up with Greg as he got out of the elevator, holding a Styrofoam cooler. I grabbed him by the elbow, spun him around and pressed the button to take us back down to the morgue.

"Where are we going? I stopped off at Bobby's already for extra blood," Greg said as the doors slid shut.

I raised an eyebrow at him.

"This seems like a tough job, and I don't want us to run out. And I thought Sabrina might have some family crap to deal with. Just trying to be helpful."

Every once in a while, like once a decade or so, Greg surprises me with his observations.

"Fair enough," I said. "And thanks. We're going back to see Bobby. He knows more about these attacks than he told us."

The doors slid open, and we walked down the hallway. Greg kept trying to say something as we walked, but I just held up a hand. Bobby knew what was going on, and he hadn't bothered to tell me. I was pissed, to say the least.

I barged through the doors of the morgue right in the middle of an autopsy. Bobby was elbows-deep in a dead guy's midsection, and I skidded to a halt right inside the door. The smell was almost enough to knock me over, the scent of blood and decay and disinfectant making my eyes water.

"Jesus Christ, Bobby. How do you work in that stench?"

Bobby reached up and clicked off a recorder. "I'm human, Jimmy. And I put Vick's VapoRub on my upper lip for the bad ones. This is a bad one. The jar's on the counter."

I opened the jar and smeared some of the ointment on my lip. I held it out to Greg, then realized that he wasn't with me. My partner, knowing what was going on, had stopped outside the swinging doors to the autopsy room. He waved at me. I mouthed *Asshole* back at him. He waved again.

"What happened to him?" I looked at the corpse. It had been lying around for a few days getting smelly. Bobby had the midsection cut open and the front of the ribcage out.

"I think a heart attack. His mailman found him today. The mail had been stacking up for about four days, and that fits with a rough time of death. Poor dude lay there all alone, nobody to miss him but his cat."

"How do you know he had a cat?" I asked. I almost told Bobby not to answer that question, but my morbid curiosity got the better of me. Again.

"There are injuries to the soft tissues of the face consistent with a house cat," he said in his most clinical voice.

"You mean his cat ate his face?" I moved around to the head of the body. Sure enough, his eyes, lips and part of his nose were gone. There were little bite marks on his cheeks, and his earlobes looked chewed.

"Damn, dude. That's nasty," I said.

"This from the guy that drinks blood to stay alive," Bobby said.

"That's what I'm saying. My bar is pretty high, and that's nasty even to me. But I didn't come down here to talk about eating faces."

"Yeah, what's up? Greg was just here and I gave him a special deal on some extra B-negative we got in. Private donor, with instructions that his blood only be used for his transfusions. Then he died of pneumonia. Ironic, huh?"

"I guess. Tell me what you know about the faerie fights."

"The what? Oh! You mean the thing? Yeah, well, you know all about it, you said so."

"I don't know anything about it. I was lying."

"You lied to me? That ain't cool, man."

"Hello? Vampire? Bloodsucking soulless demon, remember? I lied. Now I'm not. So tell me what I want to know."

"I can't, Jimmy. They'd sic their trolls on me if I talked, and you saw what they can do to a faerie. I don't even want to think what they'd do to a human. Besides, I don't know anything. I just go to the fights, put a little money down, watch the show, you know? It's not like they're people. They're monsters."

"Like us?" Greg asked.

He'd finally braved the funk in favor of knowing what the hell was going on. I swear, curiosity might turn out to be lethal to vampires, too.

"Nah, you guys are cool. But I don't know these guys. I mean, look, I'll tell you what I can." Beads of sweat had popped out on Bobby's forehead. Even though he was a big guy, and a former professional athlete, he knew he didn't want to find out just how strong a pissed-off vampire is.

"Let's start with where the fights happen," I said.

"They move, man. I get a text with a date, and if I want to go to the fight that night, I reply 'yes.' Then I get a text with an address and a time. Never more than an hour's notice, and so far it's never been the same place twice."

"When's the next fight?" Greg asked.

"Tomorrow night. I didn't reply, 'cause I got a date with a good-looking lady, you know?"

"Reply. Tell them yes. Then when you get the location, you call me. Immediately." I leaned in and showed a little fang to drive my point home. Pun completely intended. Bobby nodded frantically, then pulled out his cell phone.

He sent off the text and looked up at me. "You gonna head out now and go do some investigating or something?"

"Not yet, Bobby. First you're going to tell me everything you know about the fights. And I mean everything."

"Okay, just . . . back up a little, would you? You're kinda crowding me a little."

"It's intentional." I loomed a little more, then backed off and sat on a rolling stool. "Speak."

"Well, as far as I can tell the fights have been going on for a couple months. They started off slow, like boxing matches, or something. But as the crowds got bigger, the fights got rougher, nastier. They had a first blood match, where the winner is the guy who makes his opponent bleed first. Then they built the cage, and it went no-holds-barred. Whatever the fighters wanted to use, they could use. That last fight, with the faerie dude? It was a damn bloodbath. That troll had lost his last two fights, but he was jacked up and ready to go. He lit into the faerie like a pit bull on a steak, then he broke out this funky spiked glove and just beat the hell out of him."

"The faerie just stood there, taking it as long as he could, but he was crushed, man. And the faerie that runs the place was *pissed*. You could tell he wanted a better fight, and the crowd did too. So after the troll pounded the faerie into paste for a little while, they did a troll match. That was a lot better."

"You know that faerie was our friend's cousin, right? And that those gloves were poisoned and almost killed him, right? And that I'm gonna—"

Greg grabbed me and pulled me back before I broke any parts of Bobby that might be useful later. Like everything.

"I'm sorry, man. I didn't even think about it like that," Bobby said.

"It's cool. Just call me with the address the second that text comes in."

"Sure, man. Sure. But what are you gonna do?" Bobby looked back and forth from me to Greg.

"We're gonna do what we do, Bob. We're gonna be monsters." I let go of his collar, and he slumped backward against the corpse. "Be careful. You've got an elbow in that guy's intestines."

Chapter 23

Fortunately for us, the day turned out to be severely overcast, so Greg and I weren't trapped in the hospital until nightfall. It was still a little unnerving to be driving during the day, so I was grateful to get home after our little chat with Bobby.

I clumped down the stairs to our apartment, tired but energized to finally be making some progress. I hung my coat and guns in the closet and headed to the fridge, even though I smelled Mike hiding in the corner.

"O, B or A?" I asked Greg.

"One of each." He said as he fired up the computer. I tossed his bags of blood on the coffee table and bit into a bag of B-negative. The cold blood wasn't terribly appealing, what with the anticoagulants and plastic taste, but I needed to fill the void. I polished off the first bag and let out a contented sigh.

"Well, Mike, you gonna say something or just lie there on my couch all night?" I said to the priest.

"You knew?" he asked, impressed.

"I'm hungry. I smelled you from the top of the stairs. Been biting your nails to the quick again?"

"An old habit I revert to in times of stress," he answered.

"And this case has you stressed? That's sweet," I said.

"I do have other things in my life, James. As much as it may amaze you, I do not live solely to be your daytime errand boy." There was an odd note in Mike's voice, but he waved aside my concerned look. "Don't listen to me. I'm just a grouchy human up past my bedtime. But I am a grouchy human with information."

"Bedtime? It's not even noon," I said.

"Yes, but I haven't been to bed, Jimmy. I was planning on getting some sleep after I knew Stephen would heal, but *somebody* needed me to talk to Anna and her coven." Mike walked over to the bar and poured himself a scotch. That was one I'd never seen before—Mike drinking before noon. But I guess if you haven't slept in a couple of days, afternoon is relative.

"Sorry about that, pal. Sometimes I forget you're human."

"I'm not sure how to take that, but I'll assume it was meant as a compliment."

"It was, and besides, Anna hates me. So did you see her?"

"No. There is this remarkable invention, Jimmy. It's called a telephone. You can use it to speak to people without showing up at their place of business looking like a disheveled wino."

I gave Mike a closer look, and he did have about three days' worth of beard going, and there was more white in it than I had ever seen before. He'd lost weight, too, and it didn't look like the healthy kind. I opened my mouth to ask him about it, but he spoke first.

"Anna and her friends have noticed an increase in magical energy in recent weeks, much of it centered north of Uptown."

"There is a disturbance in the Force," I intoned gravely. Mike glared at me so I shut up. At least Greg laughed.

"Anyway," Mike went on, "according to the witches, there has been a great deal of powerful magic in use, and by several powerful practitioners. They fear that something dangerous may be on the horizon."

I raised my hand, and Mike looked over at me. "Are we talking about slip-on-a-crack-break-your-mother's-back kind of dangerous, or raising-a-demon-to-take-over-the-world kind of dangerous?"

"They couldn't tell me," Mike said ruefully. "I think they were a little embarrassed that they didn't really understand the nature of the forces at play. Anna thinks it feels potentially very bad, but couldn't say why, and no one else sensed that much."

"That's it? There was a big pile of magic being tossed around somewhere north of downtown?" I asked.

"Uptown," Mike corrected automatically.

"You realize that those are ridiculous arbitrary labels for the same piece of real estate, right?"

The whole uptown/downtown thing always bugged me. People who grew up here, like me, called the center of town "downtown," because that's what you always call the center of town. But a few years ago, the rich folks in the middle of the city decided that it should be called "uptown." So now there's all this confusion about what to call an area of like eight square blocks. But this is the same town where you can stand at the intersection of Queens Road and Queens Road, so what do you expect?

"No matter what you call the neighborhood, the disturbance seems to emanate from the industrial district between downtown and the arts district on North Davidson Street. But it moves around some." Mike rattled his glass and looked at me meaningfully.

I motioned for Greg to fix him another scotch. "All righty, then. There's a gallery crawl tomorrow night, so let's go out among the hippies and freaks to see if we can turn over a rock and find a troll underneath," I said. "If there's something going on up there that needs juice, there will be plenty of souls running around to siphon off of."

"Good idea," said Mike. Before I could find the sarcasm in his apparently sincere comment, his phone rang.

"This is Michael," he answered .

As soon as I heard the voice on the other end, I was on my way to the closet to grab my guns and coat. I put the Glock in my shoulder rig and strapped my Ruger LCP to an ankle holster. As I was pulling on my coat, I tried to listen to the conversation between Mike and Sabrina.

"He . . . it's back!" I heard Sabrina through the phone.

Greg bolted for his room to gear up as well, while Mike talked to Sabrina.

"It's beating the hell out of the cop in the hallway, and then it's coming in here for Stephen! Get away from him, you son of a bitch! No, Alex!" I heard a series of gunshots, then nothing.

I bolted for the stairs, yelling back at Mike, "Wait for us here. Tell her we're on our way."

We dashed up the stairs and jumped in Greg's car. He jammed the hot rod into gear and tore out of the cemetery parking lot like a bat out of hell. I just hoped we weren't too late for Stephen. Or Sabrina.

Chapter 24

We beat the cops to the scene, and didn't bother parking. We just pulled up to the curb and ran for the stairs. I was out of the car before it stopped—rolling awkwardly toward the building—and springing up at a dead run. And when we run, we *move*. I didn't really stop for the door, just ripped it out of the frame and ran up the three flights of stairs to Stephen's floor. I was about to rip that door off the hinges, too, when Greg grabbed my arm.

"What?" I snarled at him. My fangs were fully out, and I was in full-on attack mode. Greg pulled back a hair, but he held fast to my arm.

"Chill for a second. We don't know what we're getting into out there," he said.

"There's a troll out there, and it's come for Stephen. Sabrina's in there. I don't want it to get either of them, so I'm going to stop it," I said and tried to turn back to the door.

Greg held me still without a problem. Truth be told, he's a lot stronger than me, and I'm really strong. We've never known why some of our powers are stronger in one of us than the other, but that's the way it is.

"Dude," he said firmly. "You need to chill for a second. She's a trained professional, she can take care of herself. What if there are already cops out there? You go out there all vamped, and we've got way bigger problems than just a troll. And all you brought was guns? You know you can't take a troll out with bullets. I grabbed this for you." He handed me the sword I'd brought back from Faerieland, the one Milandra thought I might need.

"Thanks. All right, I'll go out—" Just then a huge crash from the hall shook the entire building, and we heard an enormous bellow of rage from the other side of the door. "Screw that, I'm going troll-hunting!" I flung the door open and found myself face to face with . . . Stephen.

But this was Stephen as I'd never seen him, and I was pretty sure Sabrina hadn't either. He had dropped whatever illusion kept him looking human, and he was a big dude. Stephen in faerie-form stood at least six foot eight inches and was cut like a professional wrestler. And I don't mean Dusty Rhodes. Homeboy was ripped, and he was covered in blood that didn't look like it was his. His back was to us, and I could see that he never learned that you could wear boxers under a hospital gown. But that wasn't what stopped me cold. That was the sight of Sabrina unconscious in the hallway with a nine-foot-tall troll barreling toward her at a dead run with murder in its eyes and green stuff dripping from its teeth.

I shoved Stephen to the side, and launched myself at the troll, sword outstretched. I crashed into the monster and buried my blade into its gut to the hilt. I saw about a foot of steel come out of the thing's back, but that didn't stop the troll from wrapping one enormous hand around my throat and punching me in the head with the other fist.

I felt knuckles the size of golf balls crunch into my head and my vision swam black. It pulled the fist back again, and I kicked out, catching the monster in the throat with one foot. It shook its head in sudden pain, and I took the opportunity to puke in its eyes and pull my sword from its belly.

It dropped me to wipe the blood out of its vision, and Greg came in from the other side. He buried a silver dagger in the troll's back, and the beast caught him in the face with a backward-thrown elbow. Greg crashed into the opposite wall, and I saw him sink through the drywall.

The troll caught sight of Stephen again, and started down the hall towards him. "Stephen! Get to the roof! We need room to maneuver!" We also needed a few seconds' breather, and I hoped he could outrun the massive creature long enough for Greg and me to recover our balance.

"Come on, partner, we aren't dead yet," I said as I pulled him out of the wall.

"Actually, we are," he said with a sickly grin. He pointed to the puddle on the floor. "You puked first."

"Strategy. I blinded him with my stomach acid," I said as we staggered to the stairwell. I heard the door to the roof bang open four floors above me. "We gotta hurry. Stephen can't hold that thing for long."

"We don't make stomach acid," Greg said, as we dashed up the stairs. Always gotta have the last word, that's my partner.

We reached the roof a few seconds later, and froze at what we saw. Stephen was there, and he was putting on a demonstration of the uncanny agility of the Fair Folk. I suddenly understood why legend had given them wings—Stephen looked like he was flying as he jumped and somersaulted over the swinging fists of the troll. The monster kept throwing punches, and Stephen kept dodging with a grace that was, well, otherworldly. No wonder the dance company kept him around.

"I bet he's amazing in Swan Lake," Greg murmured, just as awed as I was.

"What do you know from Swan Lake?"

"I'm cultured. But that's not the point. Let's go kick some troll ass."

I nodded at him, and then yelled out to Stephen. "Hey, Baryshnikov! Get over here, and bring your ugly friend!"

The faerie changed direction in midair and landed just in front of us, facing the troll. Greg and I spread out a few feet to either side of him, making a triangle facing the troll, who was readying for another charge. From thirty feet away, the monster bellowed a challenge, or at least what I thought was a really bad insult in Trollish. I bared my fangs and shrieked a scream that came from somewhere around my navel, and all of us rushed forward. Seconds before the inevitable collision, inspiration struck me and I knew how we could kill this thing and not get any more hammered than we already were.

"Go for the knees," I yelled at Greg, and we both dove under the troll's outstretched arms and rolled past the monster.

I lashed out with Milandra's sword and cut the monster's right leg nearly in two, while Greg spun around and shot out the troll's left kneecap. The troll flopped on its belly and slid halfway to Stephen, who looked around for anything to hit the thing with. I threw him my sword, and he cut off the troll's head, splattering even more green-black blood all over the roof. Stephen looked down at the headless monster lying in front of him, and promptly vomited all over its corpse.

"Feel better?" Greg asked me. "Now you're not the only one that puked."

"I told you, that was part of the plan," I protested, and then headed back to where the faerie was standing holding the queen's borrowed sword. When I got to him, I took the blade out of his hand, noticing as I did that the flesh of his fingers was blistered from touching the steel.

Just then, Sabrina burst onto the roof with a shotgun in hand, yelling, "Nobody move!" She saw us standing there, and then rushed over to wrap her arms around Stephen's waist. "Are you okay, Stevie? Did it hurt you? Where's Alex? Is he okay?"

"Alex is fine. I got him to hide in the bathroom when you ran out in the hall after the troll, then I led the thing away from my room so he couldn't get hurt. You guys got here just in time. I don't know how much longer I could have held out against it." The air around him shimmered for a second, and when it cleared he was in his human form again.

"I'm just glad you're both all right." Sabrina hugged him again, and then looked over at me. "What about you?"

"We're all right. A little battered, but nothing a little midnight snack won't cure. What about you? That looks like a nasty bruise." I reached out and gently brushed my fingers against a lump rising on her forehead.

Sabrina looked away quickly. "It's nothing. Just a lump."

"Well, make sure you get that looked at. We'd hate to have to break in another police department resource. Right, Greg?"

I turned to my partner, but he wasn't here. I looked around, and found him searching the troll's body. Greg reached into the dead troll's coat pocket and pulled out a cell phone and a business card.

He held up the phone. "That was nasty. But I bet this is going to be very useful indeed." Then he looked at the card. "Whoa." He passed it to me.

It was one of mine. Now that was weird. And disturbing. I don't give out many of the things, because of the stupid slogan Greg put on them. "Shedding light on your darkest problems." Bleh. But that narrowed the list of people he could have gotten the card from down considerably.

Sabrina walked over to him and held out her hand. "That's evidence, Knightwood. Hand it over."

Greg snatched back the card and slipped both items into his pants pocket. "No way. This is evidence, all right, but you guys can't fight this. If your people go looking into whatever is on the other end of this phone, a lot of them are going to end up hurt or dead. So we'll hang on to the phone, and we'll make the body disappear. And you'll figure out how to write this up in a way that doesn't mention faeries, vampires or trolls. Because that's what we do. Right?"

Sabrina stared at him for a minute, and I could almost see the wheels turning as she tried to come up with a way to follow police procedure and still do the right thing. Finally she said, "Right. I hate it, but you're right." She looked over at me. "When did he get to be the smart one?"

"As much as I hate to admit it, he's always been the smart one," I said.

"Fair enough, but I've got some questions about this troll attack, and we need to get Stephen back to his room." Sabrina took her cousin by the arm and led him through the destroyed stairwell door and down into the hospital.

We rescued Alex from the bathroom, and after convincing him that Stephen was fine, and swiping a couple of chairs from a comatose patient across the hall, we were all crowded into Stephen's room. Alex and Stephen sat on the bed, with Sabrina seated next to them.

Greg wedged a chair under the door, and he and I sat across the bed from Sabrina, who kept eyeballing Greg's jacket pocket like she really wanted that phone back. I scooted forward in my brown pleather hospital chair and moved to cut that off before she got rolling.

"We're all here, Sabrina. What were those questions you wanted to ask?"

"There are a few. Let's start with where did the troll come from?"

"That's an easy one," I replied. "What is Faerieland, Alex? Can I have silly questions for four hundred?"

"No, asshole. Why did it come here specifically? It seems pretty obvious that it was after Stevie, but why?"

"Maybe he was here to make sure Stephen was dead, or dying," I said. "Can you walk us through what happened when the troll first got to the hospital? I'm guessing it didn't just show up all green and rampaging. So what happened before you called us?"

"He looked human when we first saw him," Alex said.

"Yeah, he was dressed like an orderly, or a nurse. I can't tell. He was wearing scrubs," Sabrina agreed.

"He came into my room, and seemed surprised when he saw that I was awake. When I looked at him, I could see through his glamour. It was like there were two of him. One was the orderly, and that looked fake, like a ghost image. And then I could see the troll underneath that, and I freaked out," Stephen said.

"And when Stephen freaked out, the troll dropped the illusion, and all hell broke loose," Sabrina said.

"That's when some of us got thrown into bathrooms for our own safety," added a bitter-sounding Alex.

"I said I was sorry about that," Sabrina said in her least sorry voice.

"Okay, so what does that tell us?" I asked.

"It seems that the troll didn't expect Stephen to be awake, and when he was, he had to switch to Plan B in a hurry," Sabrina said.

"His Plan B sounds a lot like mine," I muttered.

"You mean 'punch something a lot?'" Greg asked.

"Yep, that pretty much defines my Plan B. And my Plan A, come to think of it," I agreed.

"But what does that tell us? And why did they come after Stevie and none of the other victims?" Sabrina asked.

"How do we know they didn't?" I felt a lump the size and shape of a brick settle in my stomach as a bunch of pieces started to fall into place.

"What do you mean?" Stephen asked.

"We don't know that they didn't go after the other victims, too, do we?" My eyes got wide as I listened to the words coming out of my mouth. "Oh shit."

"That doesn't sound good," Greg said.

"It's not. Whoever sent the troll here wanted to tie up Stephen as a loose end," Sabrina said.

I was still sitting there with my mouth flapping in the breeze as I realized what a hornet's nest we'd stirred up this time. "That means they'll be going after all their other loose ends, too."

"Oh shit," Greg said, realization dawning in his face.

"Yeah," I said. "And I bet if you give that card a good sniff it's going to smell like domestic beer and expensive cologne," I said.

"Why?" Alex asked, looking lost. "What's going on? And is anyone else going to come after Stevie?"

"Yes. They will come after Stephen again. And you too, now that you know about the trolls. The card will smell like beer because Jimmy gave it to the bartender at Scorpio, George. So since we talked to George, and we're involved in this mess, George is hopefully being held hostage until he's forced to fight in their next cage match."

"Why is that hopeful?" Stephen asked.

"Because that means they haven't killed him yet," I said. "Now if you'll excuse me, I've got to go find all the other victims and get them out of harm's way. If I'm not too late. Sabrina, I'm going to need you with me for the official authority. Greg—"

"Stay here and make sure that anything coming in the room with ill intent ends up with a bad case of the dead." My partner already had his pistol out and was checking the magazine.

"Detective," I said, holding the door for Sabrina. "We've got a town full of faeries to rescue."

We started at Scorpio, but before we got there Sabrina got a call telling us what we feared—the place had been trashed and George was missing. We pulled into the parking lot, and she badged us past the uniforms at the door. I looked around for Otto, but he was nowhere in sight. The club looked different with the fluorescent lights on, smaller and dingy instead of dark and mysterious. The carpet was threadbare, and the bar needed a good coat of varnish. None of this was noticeable when the dance floor was jumping, but in the midday cleaning lights, the whole vibe seemed a little sad.

I took off my shades gratefully as we walked past the vestibule and away from the daylight.

"You okay?" Sabrina asked.

"I'll live, but it's not exactly comfortable. Even with the cloud cover, I'm getting a nice sunburn. And it's hell on my eyes. My pupils are permanently dilated, so I can see in pitch darkness, but even the dim light out there hurts like a mother."

"Sorry."

"Can't be helped. Looks like they took out the front doors and surprised George behind the bar." There was a splatter of greenish-black fluid along the floor that I recognized as troll blood. That one was going to give the crime scene boys fits. Bar stools and bottles were strewn all over, George must have put up a good fight.

I spotted a few small holes in the bar top and pointed them out to Sabrina. She flagged them for the evidence guys and then dug into one of the holes with her pocketknife. A little fishing around, and she dug out a misshapen lead ball.

She held it out to me. "Shotgun."

"Yeah, I smelled gun oil on George last time we were here. He probably kept a twelve-gauge behind the bar." I hopped over and knelt down, coming up with a cut-down pump shotgun. I held it out to Sabrina.

She turned it and the pellet over to the crime scene guys and we moved into the office. A uniformed patrolman was already there, checking the surveillance tapes. I didn't expect him to find anything, since magical disguises play havoc with technology, and I was right. Just about the time two large shapes appeared on the tape, it started to static up. The best we got was that there were two big guys, and after some flashes that I took to be George shooting at them, the two big shapes carried a smaller shape out. Then the tape returned to normal.

"Weird. That's gotta be the attack, but it's like the attackers were tampering with the video somehow," the uniform said.

"Yeah. Weird," I agreed.

I motioned for Sabrina to follow me out, and we walked back into the main part of the bar. "We're not going to find anything here."

"No," she agreed. "These guys have been doing this for too long without notice to get caught by something as simple as a cheap surveillance system. We need to check on the other past competitors. If they're tying up loose ends, then anyone involved is in danger."

"I assume you have the addresses?" I asked.

"Yeah. I'll send uniforms to most of them, but this one is close. You drive. I'll call in cars for the other victims on the way."

"Where are we going?" I asked, opening the door to her car.

"The Arlington. You can find it?"

"Wish I could miss it." I slid behind the wheel and headed back toward downtown.

The Arlington caused quite the stir when it was added to Charlotte's skyline. In a city not known for terribly interesting architecture, a high-rise condo building with hot pink reflective glass in the middle of South End raised as much blood pressure as it did eyebrows. I'd never been inside one of the condos, and I didn't know anyone who could afford one. But apparently one of our victims was doing well for himself.

I took Freedom Drive to Morehead, then hung a left on South Boulevard to get to the fuchsia eyesore. The doorman came out waving his arms wildly and stretching his coat buttons to the breaking point when I parked right in front of the building, but one look at the gun in my hand and the badge in Sabrina's silenced any protests he had.

We took the elevator to the twelfth floor and knocked on the door of Benjamin Overcash, age twenty-six. Nobody answered. I checked the knob. "Locked." I whispered to Sabrina. "Do you have one of those cool lockpick kits like cops on TV?"

"No. Breaking and entering is still illegal on this side of reality." She pounded on the door. "Charlotte-Mecklenburg Police! Mr. Overcash, are you there?"

"Do you always have to say 'Charlotte-Mecklenburg Police' like that? Isn't that a mouthful?" I asked. "You ready for me to kick it down yet?"

"No. And yes. I mean, no, don't kick the door down. And yes, I announce myself properly every time. At least the first time." She banged on the door again. "Mr. Overcash! We believe you might be in danger. We want to help you. Please open the door."

From the other side of the door I heard a little dog barking.

"Well, he's either home or he's been taken, too. No way a man leaves his dog behind," I said.

"Does that apply to yippy little dogs, too?" Sabrina asked.

"Of course."

"That sounds like a dog crying for help to me, then. Kick it down."

I looked at her. "One day we're going to have a talk about exigent circumstances and just kicking in doors for the hell of it. For the record, I prefer to kick the doors in for the hell of it." So I kicked the door in.

And found myself staring down the barrel of a revolver held by a very angry-looking man holding a very small dog. He was a trim white guy with short blonde hair, khakis and a pale purple polo shirt. He looked just like every other off-duty bank drone in Charlotte. I peeked around the side of his head to see if I could spot the pointy ears, but his glamour was locked down tight.

"What the hell are you doing?" he asked.

"Would you believe me if I told you we were rescuing you?" I asked, snatching the gun away from him. He didn't look like he wanted to shoot me, and I didn't want him to screw up and disappoint himself.

"Most people who want to rescue me don't kick my door in," he said, backing away and pulling out a cell phone. "I'm calling the police!"

"We are the police," Sabrina said, holding up her badge. "Well, I am, anyway. This is James Black, he's assisting the department with our investigation into the attack you experienced earlier this month. Now please put the phone down and come with us. It's not safe here."

"Obviously not, with you barging in here like that. And I'm not going anywhere with you, especially now that my door has been destroyed!"

He was starting to vibrate, he was so pissed. I would have normally found it amusing, but George was missing, and I felt responsible. It was my business card that brought the trolls to him, after all.

"Cut the shit, pal. We know you're a faerie, and that it's not just a slur. We know about the fights, and the people that run them know we know. And they're tying up loose ends. Permanently," I said, stepping all the way into the apartment and closing the door behind me.

Overcash turned as pale as a vampire as he processed what I was saying. He stood stock still for about ten seconds, then thrust the dog into my arms and said, "Hold Phoebe." Then he turned and sprinted into what I assumed was a bedroom. He came back seconds later with a duffel bag in his hand and a backpack across his shoulders. He took the dog from me, took a look back into his apartment, then sketched a circle in the air between us. A glowing portal opened up, he stepped through, and Benjamin Overcash, age twenty-six, was gone.

"Is there anybody in the world except me that can't cast spells?" I asked Sabrina.

"I'm still just a lowly human. You're not completely outclassed by the cosmos yet," Sabrina said. "On the bright side, I don't think we need to worry about Mr. Overcash's safety."

"True enough. But he didn't give us any information we could use. Where are we headed next?"

I pulled the door closed as we left the apartment and headed for the elevator. Sabrina started calling the uniforms she'd assigned to the other victims. Just as we got in the elevator, my pocket buzzed.

My cell was thankfully intact after my trip across dimensions, and I read the screen. "Well, shit. You can hang up now," I said to Sabrina.

"Why, what's up?"

"Just got a text from Greg. Bobby called him to say that the announcement for tonight's bout just went out. No location, but on the card is a twenty-person battle royal featuring all their former competitors plus a host of special guest combatants."

"Son of a bitch."

"Yeah. So it sounds like they've gotten their hands on most of the victims already."

"And I can just guess who they want for their special guest fighters," Sabrina said as we got out of the elevator.

"Well let's get everybody together at our place and figure out how to ruin their plans."

"You drive, I'll gather the troops," she said, throwing me the keys.

Chapter 25

Two hours later there were six of us crowded into our increasingly cramped living room, sitting around the coffee table drinking the last of the coffee and watching Greg try to hack the encryption on the troll's smartphone. Who gives a troll a four-hundred-dollar phone, anyway?

"You got anything?" I asked again.

Greg had been trying every trick in his MacBook to break into the troll's phone, but couldn't come up with the password. "No. Still. And the more times you ask, the less likely I am to be able to concentrate on this and actually do anything," he snapped.

"Sorry. Sounds like Mr. GrumpyPants got up on the wrong side of the coffin tonight," I muttered.

"You don't really sleep in coffins, do you?" Stephen asked, a little confused.

"Seriously? Dude, are you really six inches tall with wings and a tiara?" He ought to know better.

"Well, I do have a tiara, but that's a long story," he joked.

"I got it!" Greg suddenly shouted.

"Got what?" I asked.

"The password. I got it. Sorry it took so long, but there are a *lot* of random five-digit numbers. Now all we have to do is look at his inbox and see who the last few text messages are from, and we should be able to go from there."

Greg pressed a few more buttons, plugged in another cable that I didn't recognize and a list of text messages popped up on the TV.

"Who has he been texting?" Sabrina asked.

"Well, there have been seven text messages since we killed him, all escalating in intensity. The last one reads 'Where r u? Got to go tonight! Must have package. Contact me immediately.'"

"Awesome. That fits with my plan perfectly," I said.

"You want to share with the rest of the class?" Sabrina asked.

"Yeah. We pretend to be the troll and find out where he was supposed to take Stephen. Then we show up instead and bust the bad guys," I said.

Greg nodded and started typing on the phone's small keypad, sending a reply to the phantom boss.

"Wait a sec." I handed him my cell. "Use this one. Tell him the troll's old phone was wrecked in the fight and he just got a replacement."

"Good idea," Greg said. He took my phone and started typing. "Sorry 4 delay," he wrote. "Trouble @ hospital. Phone busted, just got new 1. Got package, send delivery address."

"What do you mean? Sent yesterday!" was the immediate reply.

"Phone wrecked. Need address," Greg typed after a second.

"I thought that's what you had Bobby for." Mike said.

"Bobby never gets the location until an hour before the show. If we can get there earlier, there should be less chance of civilians getting hurt."

A reply flashed on the screen. "1431 Toal. Be there by 11, show starts @ midnite."

I looked at the clock—7 P.M. "Okay," I said. "We've got four hours to get there, recon the place where the 'show' is supposed to take place, figure out what the 'show' is, and ruin everybody's entertainment for the evening."

"Well, I can help with some of that before we leave," Greg said, typing more on his laptop. A new screen popped onto the TV with an aerial view of the address from the text message. "It's not exactly NSA-quality stuff, but Internet maps and satellite views will at least give us an idea of cover and entrances and exits before we get there."

"And keep us from getting a nasty surprise," I finished his sentence.

"Exactly." Greg said. "Now, it looks like this street makes a loop, and the warehouse in question is set a little back from the main road. We have loading dock doors on the right-hand side, and office doors on the front of the building. I don't have a decent view of the back of the warehouse, but let's assume that the traffic is going to be coming in from the loading dock."

"Why would you assume that?" Mike asked.

"Because it's hard to carry an unconscious person through a single door. Don't ask me how I know that," I replied.

"Right," Greg agreed.

I stepped in and grabbed the mouse, using it as a pointer. "If we park here and here," I indicated a couple of buildings around the corner from our target, "then Mike and Alex can keep the exits to the office park covered in case there are runners. Stephen and I will go in from the loading dock, while Sabrina and Greg slip in from the front entrance."

"Why am I going in the back way?" Sabrina asked.

Greg spoke up with a grin. "Because Jimmy and Stephen are better suited to a frontal assault. You're not as fast or as strong as either of them, so you should try for the sneak attack. I'm not the most stealthy, obviously, but I can keep my mouth shut, and Jimmy can't, so he has to go in guns blazing."

I didn't dignify my partner's insult with a response. Besides, he was right.

"Okay, everybody make sure you're armed enough." I stood up and lifted the lid off the coffee table.

Under the tabletop was a cleverly disguised gun safe, with room for half a dozen shotguns and rifles, plus a dozen or so handguns. I went to the coat closet and put my guns back on, double-checking my ammo situation. I hadn't fired a shot in last night's encounter, but it's always worth another peek before you leave the house under-armed. Greg had a Glock identical to mine in a shoulder holster and a Mossberg shotgun. Sabrina had her department-issued Smith & Wesson .40 in a shoulder rig, and I saw her pick up a Glock 19 from the case and clip that onto her belt as a backup.

"I don't really know much about guns," Stephen said tentatively, obviously unnerved by the amount of ammo and gun oil floating around the room.

I handed him a belt with a couple of long daggers in it and said, "Use these for anything close. Grab that shotgun and point it in the general direction of anything you want dead. The buckshot will take care of the rest."

He still looked a little shaky, but better nervous than dead. Mike, as usual, declined the use of a gun, but Alex picked up a .38 revolver, checked the cylinder expertly, and tossed a couple of speed loaders in his jacket pocket.

I raised an eyebrow, and Alex laughed at me. "Remember, Mr. Black, faerie, not pansy. I know my way around a pistol."

"Noted." I chuckled. All geared up, we split into separate cars and headed out for a little party crashing. Just before I walked upstairs, I reached back into the closet and grabbed Milandra's sword. It had come in handy once already. No sense in leaving it behind.

Chapter 26

We got to the meeting place and split up according to the plan. Stephen and I got into Greg's car and rolled slowly into the parking lot, while Sabrina and Greg went in the front door on foot. Not for the first time, I wished for those snazzy in-ear two-way radios that you see on all the cop shows, but as it was, we just made sure our cell phones all showed roughly the same time, and went for it.

The big roll-up door at the loading dock was open, with a pair of trolls flanking the opening. These guys were decked out in full leather armor, with chain mail pieces, helmets, giant battle-axes and war paint. It looked like some comic book version of what a troll warrior was supposed to look like. They would have seemed ridiculous if they weren't nine feet tall with axes that gleamed in the streetlights.

I got out of the car and walked up to the steps beside the dock, Stephen in tow. The smarter-looking of the two trolls (and let me tell you, that's a race to the bottom if I've ever seen one) held out a hand and reached behind his back. I tensed and put a hand on my Glock, but relaxed when he brought out an iPad.

"Are you on the list?" he rumbled. In his giant mitt, the iPad looked like a Barbie phone, but he managed to scroll down a list of members or something.

"Probably not. I brought the faerie you've been looking for." I gestured back at Stephen, who did that shimmer thing and revealed his true form. "Let me talk to your boss."

"No way, vamp. Give us the faerie, and we won't crush your head. But you don't get to see the boss."

The dimmer-witted troll was looking very confused by all this talking, and he started forward, axe in hand. His partner waved him back and said, "Gorton wants to smash you. Give me the faerie, and I won't let him."

"As much as I appreciate you looking out for my well-being, I think I'll pass. Now call your boss and I won't blow off anything you're fond of." I pulled my Glock and pointed it at an area just south of his belt buckle.

He got the point, but his friend Gorton didn't. As soon as he saw the gun, he raised the axe and charged. Stephen suddenly got over his fear of firearms and put five shells of double-ought buckshot in the troll's chest. It went down in a spray of green flesh and black blood, axe clattering across the pavement. That wouldn't kill a troll, no matter how much I wished it would, but he'd be out of the fight.

"Now," I said, keeping the Glock trained on the other troll's most prized possession. "About that whole 'seeing the boss' thing?"

He looked over at Gorton, then back at the pair of us, and motioned for us to follow him into the warehouse. Since no one else had come running when Stephen went all Rambo on the troll, I figured Sabrina and Greg had taken care of the other guards. I nodded to Stephen, who had finished reloading, and we walked into the dark warehouse after the troll.

I paused just outside the door to listen for heartbeats, breathing, guns cocking—anything that would give away that somebody on the other side of the door was going to put a couple rounds in my head as soon as I crossed the threshold, but I heard nothing. Our guide led us through a maze of shelving to a big open area where a cage had been set up with bleachers and lights all around it. I looked around in confusion, trying to reconcile the arena-sized interior of the building with the warehouse-sized exterior.

Stephen saw my puzzlement and chuckled. "Magic, Jimmy. The building is bigger on the inside than on the outside."

"How?" I asked. "That doesn't make any sense."

"I did mention magic, didn't I? It never makes any sense except to the spell caster, and they're all a little bit crazy. Keep your eyes open. This is going too well."

"That's what I was thinking. I hope the others are okay." Just then the troll reached the far wall of the open area, and knocked on a door. The door clicked open, and he gestured for us to go inside.

"Boss is in there. I gotta go help Gorton pick buckshot out of his lung. That wasn't very nice, shooting him." He looked at Stephen reproachfully.

"It wasn't very nice of him to try to cut me in half," Stephen replied calmly.

"He's not very smart. He saw guns and got angry. It happens." The troll shrugged a shoulder the size of a VW bug and walked past us back the way we came.

I looked at Stephen, who looked back at me and shrugged himself. That seemed to just about cover the situation, so I shrugged back at him, and walked in the door.

We stepped into an office that looked nothing like anything I expected. It looked more like a cross between a library and an armory, with melee weapons of all shapes and sizes on stands and on hangers all over one wall, all showing signs of heavy use. Two walls were taken over by floor-to-ceiling bookshelves, filled with old, leather-bound books. The books also showed signs of heavy use, and the room even had one of those rolling ladders on a track circling three walls to provide access to the upper shelves and the highest weapons.

The fourth wall was taken up by a bank of flat-screen televisions, some showing news feeds, some showing movies, and several showing closed-circuit security camera feeds from around the building. I pointed to one screen that showed Gorton lying on the loading dock while his compatriot picked buckshot out of him with a pocketknife. Of course, a troll's pocketknife would be a human short sword, so it wasn't a simple operation. Somehow I still couldn't find it in myself to feel bad for the guy. Especially since another screen showed half a dozen terrified men in their twenties crammed into a cage half-naked and dressed like extras in *Spartacus*.

Seated in one luxurious chair in front of the bank of television screens was the last thing I would have expected. Sipping on amber liquid from a crystal glass was a faerie. He wasn't nearly as good-looking as the other faeries I had met. He had pinched features, beady dark eyes, and slightly greasy hair pulled back into a tight ponytail, but he was unmistakably a faerie. The chiseled jawline, ridiculously high cheekbones and angular slant of the eyes would have been clues even if I hadn't seen the pointed ears right away. He looked a lot like someone took everything that made the Fae so annoyingly attractive, and then dropped those features on a third-string mobster. *Great*, I thought. *We get to bring down the Joe Pesci of the faerie world.*

I didn't say anything, and neither did Stephen. I just walked over to the wet bar behind his little seating area, poured myself a drink, and took a seat. Stephen passed on the drink, but sat in a chair off to one side.

After a long few moments, our host finally looked over at us and said, "You two have cost me a great deal of money, and two trolls. That bill will have to be settled." He looked at me and his dark eyes glittered. "I have heard of you, vampire. I am not impressed."

"Sorry to disappoint. If I'd known I was meeting fans today, I would have put on clean socks." I finished my drink. "Nice scotch. Now, time to shut down your little fight club."

"Or?" One greasy Fae eyebrow shooting north almost to his receding hairline.

I've always wanted to be able to do that, but regardless of the hours spent practicing in the mirror, I can never get only one eyebrow to go up. So instead of looking bemused, or sardonic, or some other fifty-cent word, I just end up looking surprised.

"There's no 'or,'" Stephen answered while I was contemplating eyebrows. "Just stop. Simple as that."

"Well, my dear ballerina, I fear there is nothing simple about it. You see, gentlemen, I make a great deal of money from our little enterprise here, and as I rather like money, and what it can buy me, I doubt I'll just decide to stop out of the goodness of my heart. Besides, I enjoy it." He leaned back in his chair, and picked up a remote control. "Take a look. You might find yourself hooked."

He pressed a few buttons on the remote, and the lights in the room dimmed. A projection screen lowered from the ceiling, and images flickered to life.

We sat there as a greatest hits montage of faerie/troll combat rolled across the screen. I recognized all the beating victims in one state of combat or another, from standing triumphant over a fallen troll to bouncing off the canvas with blood oozing from eyes, ears and mouth. In every shot one thing was constant—the crowd was going absolutely nuts. No matter who won, the crowd screamed with a frenzy that one usually only sees at NASCAR crashes.

Our host spun his chair back around and looked levelly at us. "As you can well imagine, there is a significant amount of money wagered on these events. And no matter who wins the fight, the real winner is always the house. As I am the house, I do not intend to give up that revenue stream. So it seems we are at an impasse. And if you are not here to fight in tonight's event, it seems I must recruit another combatant."

"Like your monster tried to 'recruit' me?" Stephen spat.

"Precisely. Given our kind's recuperative capabilities, had you been a little less resistant, we could have knocked you unconscious, brought you here and put you through a full bout without anyone ever being the wiser. Now look at all the problems you have created." He put down his glass and steepled his fingers. "What could I ever do to convince you that it would be in your best interests to participate in tonight's event? Oh, I have an idea."

I didn't like the sound of that. I hate it when the bad guys have ideas. I hate it even more when they smile about those ideas. Our nameless little friend picked up his remote again, and the screen withdrew back into the ceiling. On the center monitor was exactly what I was afraid I'd see—an image of a troll carrying an unconscious Sabrina in through the loading dock door.

Our host looked up at us, wearing a smile colder than the winter wind outside, and gestured to the weapons lining the walls. "Choose your weapons, gentlemen."

Chapter 27

Stephen drew both daggers and started for the faerie behind the desk, but I held him back. "I don't think that's going to do your cousin any favors."

"Quite correct, Mr. Black. What *has* this world come to when a bloodsucking fiend is the voice of reason? Now, Stephen, our bout begins in just a few hours, so I suggest you go to the locker room and join your compatriots. I have something very special planned for tonight's event. Have you ever seen a *real* battle royal, gentlemen? Not the silly things on your wrestling programs, but a real fight to the death? I think in this case it will be more like twenty men and trolls enter, no one leaves. How does that sound?" He leaned back and smiled again, reaching for his glass.

His hand never got there. He froze as an enormous crash echoed through the warehouse. Gunshots and screams rattled the walls as the cavalry appeared on the monitor. Greg was a blur on the screen, blasting his way through a horde of trolls on his way to rescue Sabrina, who had "suddenly" regained consciousness and was steadily shooting holes in the trolls nearest her.

Our oily friend reached into his pocket, but I was behind the desk with one hand on his wrist and the other lifting him by his throat before he could withdraw his hand.

"Take your hand out of your pocket. Very slowly. And if it's not empty, I'm going to rip it off and drink you dry from the shoulder."

He looked down at me, and I don't know if it was the fangs or the look in my eye that convinced him, but he complied. I was a little disappointed, having developed a taste for faerie blood over in Never-Never Land. I looked back at the monitors, then at Stephen. "Go ahead, kick a little troll booty of your own. No point letting the cop and the bloodsucker have all the fun."

He ran out to join the fray like a kid running into the living room on Christmas morning. I wondered for a second how his new bloodthirst was going to go over with the other guys in *Nutcracker*, then turned my attention to the matters at hand.

I dropped the faerie into his chair and sat on the edge of his desk. "So your guys fell for the noisy decoy and missed the stealthy fat vampire. I think you need to buy a better class of henchman next time. But now that we're alone, I don't have to be nice."

"I wasn't aware that you were on your best behavior when you threatened to rip my arm off." He rubbed his throat.

"If I wasn't on my best behavior, I wouldn't have given you the option to keep the arm." I knocked back the last swallow of his scotch, then continued. "What's your name?"

"Not that I owe you anything, vampire, but I am called Leonard."

"Okay, Lenny, who's your boss?"

"I am."

"You know I can hear your heartbeat, right? I know when you're lying." I leaned in like I was listening close. "Yup, big old fibber. Now let's try this again." I punched him in the chest, cracking a couple of ribs in the process. "Who. Is. The. Boss?"

He coughed hard, and rubbed his chest where I'd just left a handprint as a souvenir. "I run the show here."

"That's not what I'm asking," I said, as I backhanded him, hard. Both lips split and a thin line of blood arced out to splatter on the desk blotter. "I'm going to run short on time soon, because my friends don't approve of me beating people up. So stop dancing around, and just tell me what I want to know."

This time I punched downward, breaking his nose and sliding it sideways across his face. Blood poured down the front of his shirt, and I was really starting to have trouble not eating him when I heard him mumble something.

"What?" I said, yanking his head up.

He grinned at me, his face a mask of blood.

"What's so funny?"

Unable to talk, he stretched out a hand and pointed behind me. I turned, and let his head drop as I caught sight of the monitors. The fighting was all over, with Stephen joining Greg and Sabrina in high-fives and touchdown dances with unconscious and wounded trolls scattered all around them.

But of course that wasn't the only thing on the monitors, and it wasn't the most important thing, either. In the center monitor, coming through the front door, was a pair of faeries that looked like stereotypical martial arts movie bad guys. They had the long ponytails, long coats, no shirts, and most importantly, they had pistols pointed at Alex and Mike's backs.

"Crap." I let go of Lenny's ponytail.

His head bobbed loosely for a second before he regained control of himself and stood up. He was recovering pretty quickly—I guess faeries do heal fast.

"Crap, indeed, vampire." He turned his head to the side and spit a gobbet of blood onto the floor. "Now I'm going to have to clean the carpets. Do you know how hard it is to get blood out of carpets?"

"You should ScotchGard. And yeah, I know exactly how hard it is to get blood out of carpets. Try hardwood sometime. You never get everything out of the cracks." I got a smile out of him with that at least.

Then I realized that he wasn't smiling because I was funny, he was smiling because he had a very large pistol pointed at my chest.

"Have you ever wondered whether anything other than a wooden stake through the heart could kill you, vampire?" he asked with a nasty grin.

Then he shot me in the left leg, and I went down like a scrawny sack of potatoes. I lay writhing on his floor for a minute before I looked up at him and said, "This isn't going to help with your cleaning bill."

"I'm pretty sure they'll give me a rate just to do the whole room." Still smiling, he shot my other leg, this time through the calf, because I was hunched over my thighs.

It felt a lot like I'd imagined getting shot would feel. In other words it hurt. *A whole lot.* It felt a little bit like getting smashed in the leg with a hammer, if the hammer drove a burning coal all the way through my leg.

Lenny used one foot to roll me over so I was lying flat on my back. He put his boot on my right shoulder to hold me in place, and then sighted along the barrel.

"Now," he said, "I asked you if you'd ever wondered whether anything other than a wooden stake through the heart could kill you. I mean, legends are old, and there probably weren't guns when the legends first came about. So maybe we just need to conduct a scientific experiment. I know! I'll shoot you, right through the heart, and if you heal, then it will take a wooden stake. If you die, then the legends are wrong."

He stretched out his arm, and I thought about how many vampire legends were wrong—garlic, holy water, churches—all that stuff dead wrong. Sunlight did in fact burn like a champ, but we'd never experimented with the stake or fire thing. Same with decapitation—we just figured those killed pretty much anything, so no reason to think we were exempt. Now it looked like I was going to find out the hard way.

The greasy little faerie reached up, crunched his nose back into place, spat another big glob of blood onto my shirt and then shot me right through the heart.

Chapter 28

I woke up hanging from the ceiling of the warehouse, hurting in places I wasn't even really sure were places. The room was dimly lit, and smelled like old blood and rust. I tried to look around, but moving my head made me want to puke, and I thought that barfing while swinging from my wrists might be a bad idea. And it certainly wasn't going to do any favors for my poor wardrobe, which was already blood-soaked and perforated.

When I was finally able to lift my head, I saw Greg hanging opposite me, with Stephen also swinging from the rafters across the room. Sabrina and Mike were tied back to back on the floor, and Alex was tied to a folding chair. All of them looked to be in some state of disrepair, and I had a brief flash of fierce pride in my friends knowing that we didn't go down easy.

I heard the rumble of a crowd outside the room we were in and knew we were still backstage at fight night. We weren't in the room I'd seen on the monitors with the other faeries in it, so we still had to find and free them as well as ourselves.

"Good, he's awake," Greg said. "This would be a good time to tell me you have a plan." He looked like someone had taken a baseball bat to his face, with one eye swollen shut. His mouth wasn't really working all that well, so he was a little hard to understand.

Before I could come up with something witty to say, Mike looked up at me and said "I'm sorry, James. I blew the whole operation. They appeared out of nowhere, and I couldn't fight them. I ruined everything. I'm sorry."

Mike actually looked in the best shape of all of us, even though his face was red from shame. It looked like the bad guys hadn't wasted much energy on the humans, concentrating the beatings on Greg and me. Even Stephen looked pretty fresh, although his lip was swollen and there was a splash of blood down the front of his shirt. Sabrina was sporting the beginnings of a black eye, but otherwise just looked really mad.

"Don't sweat it, Dad. I shouldn't have had you stationary. It was dumb on my part. You and Alex should have been circling the business park, not sitting still."

"But another vampire would have heard them coming," he said.

"Yeah, but I'm kinda short on vampire friends, so I gotta go slumming with humans." I laughed at my own joke, and the laugh started a coughing fit. The coughing fit racked my chest until after about half a minute of coughing and spitting up blood I heard the plink of a piece of bullet bounce off the concrete floor. "That's better. Lead tickles when it comes up, did you know that?" I asked no one in particular.

Lenny stepped out of the shadows and responded, "I've heard something about that. Well, vampire, now you know that getting shot in the heart won't kill you."

"Now it's time to find out if the same is true for greasy faeries," I said, spitting a gob of blood on his expensive Italian loafers.

He calmly pulled a handkerchief out of his breast pocket, wiped off his shoe, and then kicked me square in the balls. My vision went white from the pain and I tried my best to curl up into a ball, which is really hard when you're hanging from your wrists with your feet dangling six inches off the floor. Who would have thought the little chump could kick so high?

"I think we're past insults, don't you?" he said when I was able to focus my eyes on his face again.

"Not at all. You're still ugly and your mother dresses you funny."

Sabrina cut in before I could speak. "You know I'm a cop, and you know that this place will be crawling with police in a matter of minutes. If you're lucky, they'll just put you behind bars. It'll go easier on you if you surrender now."

"It'll go easier on you if you just keep your stupid whore mouth shut like cattle should, you human trash." Lenny was in front of Sabrina before I saw him move, and he had a knife tracing a thin line of red along her stomach.

She didn't make a sound, just gritted her teeth against the pain and closed her eyes tight. I thrashed against my bonds, rage blinding me to my pain for a moment.

"Come here you little shit, I dare you. Come on, greaseball. Try that shit with someone as strong as you!" I bellowed, then Lenny was back at me, jabbing the knife into my guts and twisting.

The last thing I heard before I passed out was a cold voice whispering, "There is no one as strong as me, little vampire. No one."

When I came to again, the smarmy little faerie was still there, grinning like a cat with a spare canary.

"Now would you like to hear my proposition, or should we just trade barbs and torture all night?" Lenny asked.

"Which one is going to hurt more?" I asked.

"Well, one has the potential for great pain, while the other has the certainty."

"Then why don't we go for 'potential' for a change? I'd hate for you to get bored with torturing me."

"Oh, don't give up on my account. I have a great deal of patience when it comes to torture."

"Oh good lord, will you can the witty repartee and move on to the monologue already," Greg yelled.

I closed my eyes as Lenny crossed the floor to face my bleeding partner.

"I'm sorry, vampire, I don't think anyone was talking to you."

"Oh, come on. We've all read the comic books. This is the point where you tell us your diabolical plan for world domination, so we can come up with some clever and unexpected way to stop you." Greg looked down at the greasy faerie. "It's a formula thing, just go with it."

"Well, Mr. Knightwood, I hate to disappoint, but I have no aspirations to rule the world. I just want to make a lot of money. And you fine people are going to help me."

"I doubt it, assclown," Sabrina said.

"Detective Law, didn't anyone ever teach you to shut up when the more evolved species are speaking? It's better for your health and you might learn something."

Lenny took two long steps to where Sabrina and Mike were sitting and slapped her hard across the mouth. She rocked back and I saw blood coming from her split lip.

"You done beating up humans and defenseless vampires, or are you going to prove your sexual inadequacies a little more fully before you make your offer?" I said. I didn't really *want* to get kicked in the balls again, but better me than Sabrina or Mike.

He turned to me, glaring. "Here is what's going to happen, Mr. Black. My card starts in thirty minutes. I have a few warm-up matches, some troll on troll violence, a few faerie volunteers, that sort of thing. Then, just as the crowd is building to a fever pitch, you are going to go out there and fight a troll in a cage match to the death. These people have never seen a vampire before, so I can substitute that as a main event and not have to refund anything.

"If you win, everyone here goes free. All the faeries, all your stupid human friends, everyone. If you lose, well, you won't care very much in that case, now will you?"

"What about your battle royal? Why would you keep your word if Jimmy wins?" Greg asked.

"You mean when I win, right partner?" I asked through a mouthful of blood.

"Sure, whatever. But why should we trust the ugly fairie?" Greg asked.

"Because you have no choice," Lenny said. "You're my captives, and if I want to kill you, I can. But I'd rather see you fight. I make more money that way. And you bleed longer. Now, what's it going to be, vampire? Are you going to play the lone hero, or do I start killing the humans?"

Chapter 29

The crowd was rabid as I walked to the ring. The spells cast to make the warehouse bigger on the inside than the outside were in full effect here. There was a whole damn arena set up. There was a lighting rig worthy of ESPN, aluminum bleachers like you see at every high-school football field in America and a round cage with eight-foot chain link walls, just like on TV. Except on TV the metal poles holding the cage together were covered in padding with sponsors' logos on them, not barbed wire.

I was dressed in clean clothes that Lenny had brought over from our place. Too bad faeries don't have the same breaking and entering restrictions as vampires. He had taken the time to feed me, and since he'd ordered his faerie ninja bodyguards to let me drink from them, my wounds had pretty much healed.

I looked across the ring, and standing there with a battle-axe in each hand was my old friend Gorton the troll. He looked pretty healed, too, and pretty grumpy with me. I was unarmed, except for my teeth and my wits, which basically meant that I was unarmed.

Lenny walked into the center of the ring, and a microphone descended from the rafters. "Ladies and Gentlemen, welcome to Fright Night Fight Night!"

The crowd actually cheered for this crap, proving that there really is no relation between taste and cash.

"We have a very special treat for you tonight, a battle of legendary enemies, creatures whose races have hated each other since before the dawn of human history. The hatred that these monsters bear for each other makes Jon Stewart and Pat Robertson look like bosom buddies!"

The crowd laughed again, and I looked over at Gorton, trying to see if he had any deep-seated hatred I hadn't noticed in our first meeting. He just looked back at me as if to say *what can you do, he's got the microphone and is nuts besides.* I turned my attention back to the faerie with the microphone, thinking how much I'd rather have him locked in the cage with me than the troll.

Lenny went on. "In this corner, we have your champion, the hero of the cage, the Green Machine—Gorton the Troll!"

Gorton raised his arms above his head and played to the crowd. I could see a line of people building at what I assumed were betting windows in the back of the room.

Lenny turned to me and said, "And in this corner, hailing from right here in Charlotte, NC—the bloodsucking demon of the night, the Vampire!"

Great, I didn't even rate a name. Asshole.

"You know the rules, ladies and gentlemen. There aren't any. You have thirty seconds to place your bets, either in person or online. Wave to our audience at home, fighters." Lenny waved at the ceiling, and I noticed cameras mounted above the ring for the first time. The son of a bitch was *streaming* this?

"The betting is now closed. Let's get ready for Friday Night Fights!"

The crowd actually chanted the last bit along with him, and Lenny turned around in a slow circle, basking in their cheers. I couldn't figure out what it was—the ponytail? The earrings? The fact that the whole crowd was plastered? He wasn't any funnier than me, and I had the whole vampire chic thing on my side, but he had these folks eating out of his hand.

I looked across at Gorton, and he actually mouthed *sorry* at me. I was going to feel bad about killing him, even if he was a troll. Of course, I'd feel even worse if he managed to kill me. But since I'd technically been dead for most of two decades, I didn't mind all that much.

Gorton took a step forward, and I suddenly noticed that Lenny wasn't talking anymore. As a matter of fact, he wasn't even in the ring. I was now locked in a cage with a troll who wanted to cut my head off, and a whole bunch of people just outside that had serious cash on him doing just that. Even if I beat Gorton, I might not make it out of this alive.

I didn't have a whole lot of time to contemplate my eventual escape, because Gorton charged me, twirling his battle-axes like a Bruce Lee villain. Except they usually had nunchuks. And except that Bruce Lee could usually beat them. And except that was in the movies, and this was frighteningly real. Okay, now that I think about it, it was nothing like a Bruce Lee movie, but in the heat of the moment, that's what came into my head.

Gorton came at me in a dead run, and I sprinted away from him, running in circles around the cage while I frantically tried to think of a plan. I'm sure I looked like Andy Kaufman in a wrestling ring, but I had no idea how I was going to go toe-to-toe with a nine-foot troll and live, especially since he had two battle-axes and I just had me.

Then it came to me—I had *me*. I was a lot faster and at least marginally smarter than the troll, so that's what I had to work with. I stopped abruptly, dove backward toward Gorton and flipped over his back.

He almost turned himself inside out trying to reverse his run and get turned around to face me, and that's when I was able to snatch one axe out of his hand and fling it outside the cage. I heard a few shrieks from the crowd as the six-foot axe cleaved a bleacher, but they weren't high on the list of things I was worrying about. I guessed the people scrambling out of the way had bet on the troll.

One axe out of the way, I squared off against Gorton, who had regained his balance and was facing me head-on. He feinted once at my head, and then made a huge upward sweep at my face as I ducked. If I'd been human, that would have split my head open from jaw to eyebrows, but I left human behind a long time ago. I pulled my head back in the nick of time, and lashed out with a kick at Gorton's knee. My foot connected solidly, and I heard something go crunch. The troll didn't fall, though, just shifted his weight and brought the axe back around.

I gotta get a book on monster anatomy, I thought as I skipped sideways to avoid a huge over-handed slash that tore the canvas and splintered the wooden floor underneath.

"Careful, there, Gortie. If you break the cage it's gonna come out of your pay." I kept dodging, hoping I could rope-a-dope long enough to get a good shot in.

"What pay, vampire?" The troll asked as he slashed at my head again.

I ducked easily and rolled forward under his arm, forcing him to stop hacking at me for a minute to untangle his feet again. "You mean you're letting the faerie make all the money? That's generous of you."

"What do I need money for? He gives me blades and things to hit. That's all I need." He raised the axe over his head and charged again.

I slid sideways and gave him a couple of quick punches to where a human's kidneys would be. By the grunt he gave, I hit something uncomfortable at least.

"Don't you want more out of life? A little piece of land with a house, a yard and a Mrs. Troll in the kitchen?" I ducked another attack and this time threw a knee at the big muscle in the troll's thigh.

He yelped and backhanded me across the cage. I slid across the canvas all the way into the chicken wire walls twenty feet away, and heard people outside yelling for my blood.

"You ever *seen* a lady troll, vampire? If so, you know why I never want to get married." He came at me again, axe slashing the air at waist height.

He made a nasty sideways stroke, and I decided to do the last thing he expected. I stepped inside the axe strike, blocking his arms with my body. His elbow caught me in the midsection, but I was able to reach out and land a punch right on the tip of his bulbous nose.

I don't care how big you are, a shot to the nose is the great equalizer. Your eyes get blurry and there's nothing you can do about it for a couple of seconds. And a couple of seconds was all I needed. As Gorton reached up to grab at his face with one hand, I took his other wrist, the one closest to me, in one hand and put the other hand on his bicep. I put all my strength in one huge move, and slammed his outstretched arm across my upraised knee with a sickening pop that sounded like a huge balloon exploding. Gorton's elbow snapped like kindling, and his axe went clattering to the floor.

I held onto his wrist and pulled him around, muscles straining against his huge bulk. He overbalanced easily, going head over heels in a move I couldn't replicate if I tried it in the gym a thousand times. The troll landed flat on his back with his arms and legs splayed out wide. I picked up the axe and raised it high over my head. I looked down and saw the troll close his eyes as I brought the massive blade crashing down.

Then his eyes flew open as the splinters scratched his face when I buried the axe in the floor beside his head.

"Don't move," I whispered to the troll. Then I jumped from the middle of the ring to the upper corner of the cage, balancing precariously on the upper rails of the chain link.

"I win, Lenny, and the troll lives!" I shouted. "Now open the door. I'm hungry, and I don't really care if I eat you or one of your patrons."

I looked down at a balding man in a suit that cost more than my first car. He had a woman on each arm, obviously rentals or just run-of-the-mill gold diggers, and a Tag Heuer watch that kinda caught my eye. I bared my fangs at him, and he fainted dead away. The girls ran off, and I jumped out of the cage to land beside the fainted wuss.

"Nice watch. Thanks," I said, slipping it onto my wrist.

"That's not very nice, Mr. Black." Lenny's voice came from right behind me, and I turned to see him pointing a revolver at my head. It looked like a .357, but it was hard to tell with it pressed up against my nose.

"I'm not a very nice person, Lenny." I reached up and pushed the barrel of the gun aside. "Now open the doors. I won. My friends and I are leaving." I looked at him and put a little mojo into my voice, but it had no effect on the faerie.

"You cannot bespell our kind, you idiotic little vampire." Something in the way he said that sounded familiar, but I couldn't quite put my finger on it. "You did not win, you forfeited. That was a death match you just ruined. You don't get to change the rules. My house, my rules. And you are most certainly not leaving. I promised these people blood, and blood they shall have."

He clapped his hands, and a small army of trolls stepped forward out of the shadows. One held each of my friends and the earlier beating victims, and the ones that weren't holding prisoners held nasty-looking axes, swords and short spears with barbed points that looked like they could do really unpleasant things to people. I was happy to see that George looked like he'd held up well through the whole kidnapping into a fight club ordeal.

And then, out of nowhere, Lenny had that damn microphone again. "Ladies and Gentlemen, we have a fantastic surprise for you this evening! In addition to the bout you have just witnessed, the first time our audience has ever been exposed to a vampire's speed, grace and evil power, we have another first for you here at Fright Night—a *Battle Royal*!"

"Now this isn't the watered-down excuse for a Battle Royal that your silly 'sports entertainment' programs will show you. This is a true battle, where only the strong survive! Two teams will enter the cage, the great Warrior Trolls versus the forces of the evil vampires, and only one team will emerge victorious! But first, please step away from the cage. We need a little more room for this performance."

With that, he waved his hands in the air over his head, and the cage grew. And it didn't just expand outward, it got taller, too. What had been a fifteen-foot square with maybe ten-foot walls, was now a cage the size of half a basketball court with walls a good twenty feet high. And Lenny had transported all of us inside the cage. The spectators were outside, but Sabrina, Greg, Stephen, Mike, Alex and I were in the cage along with a bunch of terrified faeries, a bartender, a baker's dozen of trolls and one faerie magician.

I looked over at Greg. "I've got a bad feeling about this."

He nodded. "Help me, Obi-wan Kenobi. You're my only hope."

Chapter 30

We were still unarmed, and even more outnumbered than when it was just me one-on-one with a troll. I ran to the side of the cage and picked up the axe that Gorton had dropped when I felled him. He was still lying there, holding his elbow tight to his body and glaring at me, but he obviously wasn't going to be a problem. I just hoped we could end this thing before he healed and came after me. When Lenny had made the cage bigger, the other axe ended up on the inside of it with us, so I grabbed it too. I sprinted back to my friends and handed one axe to Greg.

"I figure we've got a few seconds before they figure out a plan and come after us. Sabrina, George—stay here and protect the humans. Greg, Stephen, come with me." I snapped the head off the axe and gave Sabrina the handle. It made for about a four-foot bo staff, but it was the best thing I could come up with.

I grabbed the axe just behind the head and looked over at Greg. "Fastball special?"

He looked at me and shook his head. "You read too many comic books, dude. That'll never work."

"You got a better idea?" I asked.

"No. Lie down on your stomach."

I did, and Greg grabbed my ankles and started to spin around in a circle. I held the axe head out in front of me and picked up speed with every rotation.

"I should try the hammer toss at the Ren Faire next year," Greg yelled as he let go of my feet.

I flew across the cage at the massed rank of trolls, axe-first. I hit the first one head-on with the blade, cleaving the top of his head right off. For such a stupid creature, he had a lot of brains to splatter all over the place. I kept flying into the second troll, and managed to take his head off as well before the axe handle became too slick with blood to hold.

By then Greg and Stephen had caught up with me and were picking up the weapons dropped by the dead monsters. Stephen grabbed a troll short sword that fit him like a claymore, and started laying about like a madman. I had to duck to keep him from lopping off my ears. I grabbed a fallen sword of my own. Greg had squared off against an axe-wielding troll, and was trying to chip enough important pieces off him to get him to stay down.

Sabrina, George and Mike had formed a phalanx in front of the huddled mass of frightened faeries, until a troll got too close. Once one came within a few feet of their defensive stance, a pair of men vaulted over their heads and launched themselves at the troll with a flurry of kicks and punches. These guys obviously remembered their last trip to the cage and had a score to settle. I remembered Alex's words to me earlier and grinned as I muttered "faeries, not pansies" to myself. At least for now, Sabrina, Mike and the others were safe.

I heard air whistling behind me and dropped to the ground just in time to avoid a gigantic clawed hand that would have ripped my lungs out. I lashed out with my sword, cutting the troll's Achilles tendon, and he dropped to the floor beside me. Through it all, I heard the crowd screaming for blood. Ours or the trolls, I couldn't tell.

I danced around as best I could, slicing out with my sword whenever I saw an opening, all the while trying to get back to where Greg and Stephen stood surrounded by trolls. I dove between one beast's legs, stabbing upwards through his torso as I came up, and snatched his axe out of the air as he fell backwards, dead before he hit the floor.

"How many left?" I asked Greg.

"I got two." He replied. "Stephen?"

"This one makes two for me. What about you?"

"I got three plus one incapacitated. So that leaves seven plus Lenny."

I looked around but couldn't see the faerie anywhere. It was about that time when I heard Sabrina swearing loudly. I looked over to where I had left them, only to see a troll lift her up and throw her out of the cage altogether. She landed in the crowd, and looked around for an entrance to get back in and help as the troll waded into the sea of humans and faeries, laying about with his huge fists, seemingly oblivious to the punches he was taking.

"Crap. Hold these guys," I yelled to Greg.

He nodded, and I took off across the cage with a roar that seemed to come from my toes.

The troll going after the captives didn't even look at me, just flicked out a huge fist and smashed me to the floor. I blacked out for a second or two, then came to just as the troll was swinging a sword at my head. I rolled to one side and leapt to my feet. Bad idea. I was dizzy from the punch in the head, and the troll saw it. He reared back and kicked me in the chest with one green-tinged foot. I felt a couple of ribs break, and flew about six feet before I landed flat on my back in the center of the cage.

The troll turned his attention back to the humans, and I staggered to my feet. He had just grabbed Mike around the throat and was rearing back to cave in his face with the other hand when I hurled my sword like a spear, right through the monster's back.

His hand tightened for a second around Mike's neck, and I saw his face go purple. I limped over and pried the troll's dead fingers off of him, and Mike drew a deep, raspy breath.

"Thank you, James," he said hoarsely.

"Pray for me, buddy." I shook my head to clear my vision.

Then I made my way back to the fight and tried to assess our odds. Stephen and Greg had taken out another couple of trolls, so the numbers were slowly evening up. The problem was, the remaining four trolls were in pretty good shape, and we were starting to look the worse for wear. I had a few broken ribs and probably a concussion. Greg had one arm that he couldn't move, and Stephen had a serious limp and blood pouring from a scalp wound. Plus we had the humans to watch out for.

I stepped up beside my two friends and we squared off with the remaining four trolls. They had an array of weapons to make the biggest *Dungeons & Dragons* geek envious. We had two swords, one axe, and a spectacular array of bruises.

"Ready boys?" I asked.

"Nope," Greg said.

"Not even a little bit," Stephen added.

"Good. So since none of us are stupid, what's the plan?" I asked.

"How about we kill the green guys, then we take turns cutting on the greasy faerie, and I collect my winnings," Greg replied.

"Winnings?" I looked over at him with one eyebrow raised. Apparently I can do it, but only if I'm so beaten up that half my face doesn't move.

"Yeah, I bet all my cash on you to win your match. Lenny owes me fifty grand."

"Fifty grand? How much did you bet?" I yelped.

"Two thousand. You were a pretty heavy underdog."

"No wonder he wants us dead. He doesn't want to pay you off."

"Probably," Greg agreed. "Should we start the killing now?"

"Yeah, may as well. Go for the legs if you can, the joints are the only weak spots that I've found."

"Well, that and their golf game," Stephen quipped.

"I'm the funny one," I said. "Stay off my turf, faerie."

"Bite me, vampire." He grinned and wiped a little green blood off his face.

"Tease. What would Alex say?" Then I charged, more to ensure that I got the last word than out of any real bravery.

I turned and ran straight at the nearest troll, pouring on the vamp-speed. Instead of taking another shot to the ribs, I jumped high into the air and came down behind the trolls. I cut backward through his left leg, and he fell backward onto the canvas. I sliced off his head and turned to see how the others were doing.

Greg had tangled with the biggest troll of them all, and wasn't doing so well. The troll held a huge sword in one hand, and a shield in the other, and was blocking all of Greg's axe blows with his shield, then lazily feinting at him with his sword. I didn't want to know what was going to happen when he got serious.

Stephen wasn't faring any better with two trolls all his own. One held a standard short sword, and the other a nine-foot metal-tipped quarterstaff. Stephen was fast enough to keep from getting his head crushed, but not trained enough to make headway against two opponents.

I slid in on Stephen's left and engaged the troll with the staff. He immediately caught me on the chin with his stick, and my eyes crossed again. I kept my feet, and kept moving enough not to get my head bashed in, but all I really accomplished was getting him off Stephen's back so he could fight the other monster.

Out of the corner of my eye I saw the big troll smash Greg square in the face with his shield, and my portly partner's eyes rolled back in his head as he slumped to the canvas. The troll lifted his huge sword over his head, and brought it down to chop Greg's head off in the middle of the ring.

Chapter 31

The sword met steel with an enormous bell tone, and I turned my head to see Gorton standing over Greg's unconscious body, an axe in his good hand. The other troll looked up at him in astonishment, and said something in a guttural language that I didn't understand. Gorton shook his head and barked something nasty at the larger troll, who stepped back from Greg into the center of the cage.

There was something oddly formal in the way the two trolls circled each other, then stopped, saluted with their weapons and rushed together with a clash of steel and a sweaty thump of green-hued flesh.

The monsters traded massive blows in the middle of the ring for several minutes, neither able to gain an advantage. Gorton was the better fighter, but his wounded arm evened the scale for the bigger troll, who had strength and health on his side. After three or four long minutes, it became obvious that Gorton couldn't win. He was just buying us time.

I looked over at Stephen, who had stopped fighting his troll to watch the duel just like I had. I jerked a thumb at the green brute behind him, and in unison we turned to the trolls next to us and lopped off their heads while they concentrated on the two combatants in the center of the ring.

The big troll saw what we did and flew into a rage, redoubling his attacks on Gorton. The smaller troll went down on one knee, and I rushed in to try to help him, only to run smack into an invisible wall.

Lenny floated down out of the air and said, "No interference, vampire. This is an honor match."

"I'm not really that honorable, Lenny, so get out of my way." Did I mention I hate magic? Well, I do.

"I don't think so. Be still."

He waved his arms at me and I was suddenly trapped, unable to move or lift my hands. Well, if I learned nothing else tonight, at least now I knew who was throwing around heavy-duty magic on this end of town, for all the good that would do me.

I turned my attention back to the fight just in time to see the bigger troll batter down Gorton's defenses. Gorton's axe head dropped to the floor, and the other troll reached out with one huge foot and stomped through the handle. Gorton looked up at him with a bloody smile, and the larger troll swept his head from his shoulders with one stroke. The body fell in the opposite direction from the head, blood pouring from the neck stump.

The big troll turned to me and grinned, starting to stomp my way waving his sword from side to side in a low arc. I couldn't move because of Lenny's spell. Greg was still out cold, and Stephen could barely move, he was so beat up.

I looked into the green-skinned face of my doom, and thought *this is not how I wanted to go out. Salma Hayek is not anywhere in the building.*

I closed my eyes as the troll got closer, and just as I thought I could feel its nasty breath on my face, I realized the spell was beginning to wear off. I could move, after a fashion.

I opened my eyes to see the troll standing stock still in front of me with a foot of steel sticking out of its chest. It started to fall forward, and I got out of the way the best I could. I heard a very startled Lenny mutter something very unpleasant under his breath, and looked up to see a golden-tinged dragon-man in full battle armor standing in front of me.

"Tivernius?" I gasped, baffled but grateful.

"Hello, James. Otto sent word that you had been attacked by trolls again, so Her Majesty asked me to protect her friends and her subjects."

He eyed Lenny like he was something smelly he'd stepped in. Maybe troll spleen. There was a lot of that lying around.

"Leothandron, fancy meeting you here. I thought you were banished to this realm and under strict orders to never touch magic." The dragon turned warrior put on a fake smile worthy of Joan Rivers on Oscar night. "Now what is the penalty for disobeying Her Majesty? Oh yes, I recall. Death."

With the last word, the dragon's face went cold and he closed on Lenny, sword flashing.

Lenny wasn't exactly defenseless. He conjured a pair of slim short swords out of thin air and easily parried the dragon's strokes.

"Your little bitch-queen has no authority over me here, and she knows it. If she could do anything to me she'd be here in person instead of sending her pet lizard."

Lenny slashed furiously at Tivernius' face, but the dragon saw the obvious attempt at misdirection and easily batted away the thrust that came at his midsection. He had a tougher time beating aside the next attack, which came straight at his head from both swords.

I stood there, not wanting to distract Tivernius. Besides he didn't need me. I mean, the guy was thousands of years old. He had to have learned a thing or two about sword fights, right? That comforting thought went out of my head when I saw Lenny open up a broad slash across the dragon's mailed stomach.

Lenny's black blades glowed red with blood, and the faerie smiled coldly. "You were never much of a challenge in human shape, lizard. You are only a threat in your true form, and you cannot transform in such a small building. Too bad, really. I'd love for all these people to see me beat a real dragon, instead of just another wizard."

Lenny kept fighting while he talked, a feat I had grudging admiration for. I can usually manage a one-liner or two, but this guy was positively Shakespearean.

The one thing he couldn't do was keep me bound by his magic while he fought and talked. My magical restraints vanished, and I quickly cut through the cage and got everybody out of there that wasn't already dead. Stephen protested, but I shoved him through the chain link and Alex took over from there.

I stayed to make sure Tivernius finished the job. The last thing we needed was Lenny getting away and going after his victims all over again. Plus, he'd *shot* me.

Tivernius was fast, almost faster than me, but he wasn't quite as ruthless as Lenny. The dark-haired faerie took every cheap shot he could, kicking, gouging, throwing random troll bits into the dragon's eyes, whatever he could think of to gain any advantage. It became clear after a few seconds that the combatants were pretty evenly matched, and it was all going to come down to who made the first mistake.

I couldn't get involved, because I was afraid of distracting Tivernius and getting him killed. Greg couldn't do anything, because as soon as he got everybody out of the cage, Mike and Stephen started working on his head injury. Sabrina stood beside me, coming back into the cage after reclaiming her gun. She handed me my sword belt, and I strapped on Milandra's sword. I felt a little ridiculous, but she didn't bring me my Glock.

The mistake was small when it came, just a tiny slip of a foot in a pool of blood, but it was Tivernius who made it. He lunged at Lenny after a blinding parry, and his front foot slid just a little. But that overbalanced him, and he couldn't get back in time to get his guard set.

The faerie saw it and launched a whirling counterattack that kept Tivernius off balance and backpedaling. I saw what was happening too late to do anything, as Lenny steered the dragon into the center of the cage, right where Gorton and I had finished our first scuffle.

Tivernius stepped back to avoid a slash at his throat, and put his foot right in the hole that I had made in the ring's floor. He went down clutching his knee, and his sword went flying across the cage. Lenny smiled a wicked smile and leapt up into the air, both swords flashing as he came down in a deadly strike aimed at Tivernius' sprawled form.

He never got there. As soon as I saw the opening, I launched myself at the flying faerie. Like I said, I'm fast. I was never going to make the varsity football team when I was alive, but add my vamp-strength to my ridiculous speed, and I hit Lenny in the midsection like an NFL linebacker with a bad attitude. We flew across the cage to crash into the wall, and I heard Lenny's swords clatter to the floor well behind us.

I hopped up to see the faerie already on his feet, and quickly got my head out of the way of his oncoming fist. I grabbed that wrist with one hand and threw a series of fast punches into his ribs with the other. He took my best punches without flinching, and I knew I was in trouble.

Okay, I knew I was in trouble when he took out the thousand-year-old dragon and conjured swords out of thin air, but I knew I was in real trouble when I didn't even faze him with my body shots. He did wobble a little when Sabrina put three rounds in the center of his back, but even that didn't slow him down. He quickly regained his focus. I heard Sabrina swearing from all the way across the cage. I understood the feeling.

Lenny backed away from me and squared himself up. I could almost see the wheels turning in his devious little head, and the second his hands started to wave I lashed out with a spinning kick at his head. He ducked easily, but I had disrupted his spell, so all I had to worry about was the counterattack. That was a punch to the groin that I blocked because, knowing what a dirty fighter he was, I expected the low blow. I didn't expect his other hand to stab at my eyes, but I managed to dodge back quickly enough to save my sight and my jewels.

"Nice shot. You learn to fight like that in the faerie prison?" I snarled.

He just smirked at me and flung himself at my knees. I jumped over his dive easily, and then cursed my stupidity as I saw him come out of a forward roll with a sword in his hand.

"I am the greatest swordsman the House Armelion has ever produced, vampire. You cannot best me in single combat. I will take your head, slaughter your scaled friend and your human allies and return to my homeland to wrest the throne from that lizard-loving bitch!" He advanced, his sword moving so fast the blade became a black blur whirling at my face.

"Wow, you've got some serious anger management issues. Good thing I brought backup," I said, and dove to one side.

Sabrina emptied her clip into the pissed-off faerie, which only served to distract him for a second. But a second was all I needed to come up with my sword drawn and set myself for the fight of my life.

I became a lot less set for the fight when Lenny turned to face me. His eyes were completely black, and the smile across his face was colder and crueler than anything I'd ever seen. The voice that came from his mouth was pure evil, a slithering, writhing sound that swirled around my ears and sent icicles down my spine.

"You expect to defeat me, little vampire? Do you really think you can best the greatest of the Fae? You can't touch me, fool. I was drinking babies' blood when your ancestors were crawling out of the mud and growing legs. I have waded through the gore of a thousand battles and eaten the hearts of kings. I have destroyed entire civilizations and crushed the souls of generations of men. What are you to me?"

"Well, I beat *Call of Duty 3* on Veteran. Does that count for anything? Oh yeah, and I once helped banish an Archduke of Hell. But enough about me." I lunged at him, a clumsy strike that he easily parried into a wicked slice towards my eyes.

The fight escalated into a blindingly fast exchange of thrusts, parries, slashes, dodges and curses as we both tried to grab any advantage. Sweat poured off my forehead after just a couple of minutes, and then I had the added irritation of blood in my eyes on top of fighting a more skilled opponent possessed by an undying evil spirit too evil for Hell. I called on the memory of every Saturday afternoon kung-fu triple feature just to stay alive.

After a series of whirling slashes, I saw out of the corner of my eye what Lenny was doing. He was trying his best to steer me over to the same hole he had dropped Tivernius in. The wounded dragon had managed to drag himself over to one side of the cage, leaving the hole conveniently vacant.

I spun sideways around a savage thrust and rolled forward, getting us turned around so Lenny's back was to the hole, and by the ferocity that he thrust and slashed to get us turned back around, I could tell that I was right. But try as I might to stop him, he maneuvered me around again.

If I went into the hole, nobody was left to bail me out. Sabrina was out of ammo, and everybody else was either human or injured, so I was on my own this time. I looked from side to side, frantically trying to find a way out, when Lenny caught me with a kick high in the midsection.

I screamed from the pain in my already broken ribs, and flailed my arms around like pinwheels as I stepped into the hole in the ring and went down on my back, just like Tivernius had.

Lenny grinned an evil grin and leapt into the air, just like he had over the fallen dragon. He came down with his sword ready to remove my head from my shoulders with extreme prejudice.

Except for the part where I wasn't lying there anymore. Since I knew what he was doing, I never put any weight on the leg in the hole. Instead I lowered myself backward onto the canvas in a fake fall worthy of any WrestleMania main event. When Lenny jumped, so did I, and by the time he came back down, his sword hit nothing but canvas and wood, burying itself a good foot into the floor of the ring.

Lenny looked around, startled, and his eyes got huge for a split second before I buried my fangs in the side of his neck. His blood spurted cleanly into my mouth, and I drank deep. The coppery taste of blood was mixed with the earthy taste of moss, pine trees, fresh-cut grass and late night rain in a spring wood. There was even a hint of something like mesquite before I got down to the nasty bits of Lenny, the hot anger that tasted like burned meat, spoiled cheese and a touch of churned grave dirt and tears.

I drank, and felt his hands hammer on my head and shoulders. He pounded on me like they were sledgehammers, but the more I drank, the stronger I got. His blows grew weaker and weaker. My cuts and bruises faded, and I felt my ribs begin to knit back together. Just before I took the last of his blood and turned him, I found the willpower to pull away from him, and that was the hardest thing I'd done in a long time.

I pulled back and he fell to his knees in front of me in the cage. And with him looking up at me from the brink of death and possible rebirth, I took my sword and cut his head off with one big looping stroke.

Lenny's head hit the canvas, and a black cloud of smoke billowed forth from his neck, shrieking loud enough to drive me to my knees. When I was able to open my eyes again, the body was nothing but a desiccated husk, a mummy in the middle of the cage.

Chapter 32

I closed my eyes for a long moment and let the blood flow through me, healing the hurts of my body and leaving a few more unpleasant scars on my soul. Taking in the dirtier pieces of Lenny's life force literally left a bad taste in my mouth to counterbalance the flush of healing energy I got from his faerie blood.

Sometimes I understand why Greg doesn't drink from the source anymore. Not often, but sometimes.

I looked around at the carnage and counted better than a dozen dead trolls, an unconscious vampire, a dragon with a broken leg, a bloodstained blonde faerie, a decapitated brown-haired bad guy faerie and about a dozen wary and blood-soaked humans.

Then there was me, a freshly fed monster with my opponent's blood dripping off my chin and fangs overlapping my bottom lip. The crowd stood frozen in silence for just a second after Lenny's corpse hit the canvas, then erupted in wild cheers like they had all hit the lottery.

In a way, I suppose they had, since they stormed the two trolls manning (trolling?) the betting windows and beat them with chairs, purses and whatever else they could find until the less-than-jolly green giants just threw all the money into the crowd and slunk off into the night.

I limped over to Sabrina and the others and slid down to sit in the cage with my back to the chain link. "That sucked," I said.

"Didn't look like much fun from here," she replied.

"Good. Wouldn't want you to romanticize it or anything."

"Don't worry, Jimmy. When I watch you fight, romance is the last thing on my mind."

"Yeah? Well, what does come to mind when you watch me fight, Detective?"

"The scarecrow from The Wizard of Oz on crystal meth," Greg said from where he lay on the canvas with a black bandage wrapped around his head.

"Nice. Where'd the bandage come from?" I asked.

"That would be me, James."

I looked over at Mike, who had on his priest's collar, but was now lacking the shirt that usually went with it. I couldn't help it, I started to laugh. Mike looked down at where his belly was poking out over his belt, and he laughed too. Then we were all laughing, slapping legs and the whole bit.

After a few minutes of silliness we calmed down, and looked around the empty warehouse. A few scattered dollar bills were all that was left of the cash wagered on the fight, and I swore loudly.

"What's wrong with you?" Sabrina asked.

"Lenny owed us fifty large for the first fight," I said.

She raised an eyebrow at me. "I don't think there's that much lying around."

"That's why I was cussing," I said, holding my not-quite healed ribs.

"Dude," Greg said from behind us. "I got it covered."

"How do you have it covered?" I asked.

"Lenny didn't trust all his money to the betting windows. I just grabbed about thirty grand off his dead body."

That's my partner. He might claim that I'm the money-grubber, but he's the one that'll bleed you dry. Figuratively, of course.

"Nice work, bro."

I turned to head for the exit, but stopped as the roll-up door slowly rose and a figure on a sleek black motorcycle rode in. The bike rolled up to us almost silently, and the rider pulled off her helmet as she got off and strode over to Greg.

Lilith, one-time mate to Adam the Father of Man, one-time outcast from the Garden of Eden, one-time servant to the fallen angel Zepheril and current proprietrix of the biggest and fanciest topless bar in North Carolina, strutted across the concrete like she owned the place. She was pure sex on two legs, with her leather jacket unzipped enough to make you wonder if there was anything under there, and leather pants tight enough to let you know there wasn't anything on under *there*.

"I'll take that." Lilith held out one hand for the cash.

"And why exactly would we give you my money?" I stepped in front of her. "And what are you doing here?"

"The answer to those questions should be obvious, little vampire. I'm here because this is my establishment. You'll give me the money because I now have a great deal of cleanup to do, not to mention more trolls to recruit after this debacle. Besides, you trashed my club. The money will cancel your debts to me." The immortal strip club owner held out her hand again, and I couldn't help but laugh.

"What ever happened to 'I don't know anything about the attacks you're investigating?'"

"I lied. As the scorpion said to the turtle, 'it's in my nature.'"

I got my laughter under control and said "Let me explain a couple of things, Lilith. One—we are not giving you any money. Greg won a bet, and your guys lost a fight. When that happens, you don't get paid."

She started to say something, but I reached out and put one finger across her delicious-looking lips. Lilith's lips are the reason mortal women take Botox—they're trying to catch up to what she has naturally. Too bad she knows it.

"Two—you're closed. For good. And three—"

I stopped talking because she had grabbed my finger and slid up against me, pressing herself along my body and looking up at me with a heat that I felt even without a heartbeat. She ran a finger over my lips, and I forgot how to breathe for a minute. Good thing for me it's more a force of habit than anything that keeps me alive.

Lilith looked up at me and purred "But Jimmy, I don't want to close. That would make me unhappy." She gave a little pout that made me want to give her my firstborn, my kidneys, Greg—anything to make her smile again. "And you'd much rather make me happy, wouldn't you?"

She stood up on tiptoes and licked along my jawline. I could almost feel my IQ drop into the single digits.

Suddenly Lilith flew backward and landed on her leather-clad rump, kicking up a little poof of concrete dust. I shook my head to clear it and saw a very angry Sabrina standing over Lilith with her finger in the immortal woman's face. "Look here, slut. In case you're hard of hearing as well as low on morals, the man said 'you're closed.' And I'm saying it again. You're. Closed. Any questions?"

"Oh, I understand you perfectly, Detective. But do you understand yourself?"

I've never seen anyone slink to their feet before, but Lilith moved with a liquid grace that was at the same time seductive and unnerving. Watching her walk made me wonder who was really the serpent in the Garden of Eden.

"I understand all I need to, you antique hag."

Lilith spun on her heel and stared at Sabrina like she'd been slapped.

"Yeah, I know who you are," Sabrina said. "And I know another thing—if you ever lay a finger on my cousin, or any other person in this city under my protection, I will personally end your ridiculously long life." Sabrina stood with her arms folded across her chest, almost daring Lilith to make a move.

"You can't kill me, Detective. Better women than you have tried." She turned those lethal eyelashes on me and batted them slowly. "Well, Jimmy, I could use a vampire like you. You have potential. What do you think? Money, power, and all the me you can drink? Sounds good, doesn't it?"

"Sounds yummy, except for the part where your last employee had an immortal hitchhiker wrapped around his soul. I think I'll keep my free will free, thanks. Besides, I don't go for older women," I said, stepping back from her.

I didn't know if she had anything to do with the *sluagh* infecting Lenny or not, but she didn't look surprised at the news.

Keeping Lilith at greater than arm's length was looking like a very good idea.

"Now get out of here, Lilith, and keep your nose clean. I owe you for helping us with the Belial thing, but after this, we're square. Your little fight club is out of business. Go back to running a strip bar. It's legal at least."

"Little vampire, you have no idea what forces you are setting in motion against you." Lilith stood ramrod straight, fire spitting from her eyes.

Obviously this was a woman unaccustomed to rejection. Especially from dead video game nerds.

"I do not take this insolence lightly. You will pay for the damages done here, one way or another. And you'll find that I collect my interest with extreme prejudice." Then she hopped on her bike and roared out into the night, her raven hair flying out behind her.

I heard Greg let out a long breath behind me and realized that I was holding mine as well.

"That is one scary chick," he said.

"Yeah," I agreed. "You think she knows helmets aren't optional in North Carolina?"

Chapter 33

An hour later, I was sitting on the floor of my den, leaning against a wall with a beer in my hand, looking at my friends scattered around the room and smiling. Sabrina was sitting on the floor next to me, her shoulder warm against mine. I could feel her heartbeat through her skin, pulsing along merrily. She was wearing another one of my T-shirts, her clothes having been splattered with troll blood. I was in a pair of sweats and a T-shirt, my hair still damp from a shower. I'd been covered with so much gore that I almost had to ride on the roof of my own car to get home.

Greg was in a chair pulled in from the kitchen, sipping a bag of blood from the crisper and looking better every minute. He hadn't bothered to change yet, since he was still a little dizzy from his head injury, and I told him in no uncertain terms that if he fell in the shower, he was just going to have to lay there naked until he healed, water bill be damned.

Stephen and Alex were sitting on the couch holding hands. Now that things had calmed down and no one was trying to kill any of us, Alex had a lot of questions about vampires, faeries and dragons. Stephen had more than a few questions about Faerieland for Tivernius, who sat in our lone armchair explaining what he could.

The dragon had waved his arms and all his clothes were sparkling clean again. I asked why he couldn't do that for us, and he went into a long-winded explanation that I cut off with "it's magic, you just can't." Mike walked in from the kitchen in a Batman T-shirt with a priest's collar holding a scotch for himself and one for the gimpy dragon, and sat in another kitchen chair.

"If this keeps up we're going to have to get more furniture," I said across the circle of people to Greg.

"Yeah, well, we can afford it now." He laughed, pointing over his shoulder at the pile of cash on the table.

We all chuckled, and Tivernius sipped his scotch, savoring the smoky flavor.

"I do wish we had this concoction in the lands of House Armelion," the dragon murmured.

"No scotch in Faerieland?" I asked.

"No, James, there are no fermented beverages at all in the lands of the Fae," he said.

"Well it's good to know the place isn't all purple puffy clouds, perfect weather and unicorns that poop glitter," I said.

"Unicorns do not defecate glitter, James. Whatever gave you that idea?" Tivernius asked.

"Just something I read on the Internet, pal." I laughed. Then a thought occurred to me. "Hey, Tivernius?"

"Yes, James?"

"How did you just happen to show up in the middle of the cage at just the right moment? Not that I mind, but it seemed a little more than lucky, if you get my drift."

If you've never seen a dragon blush, it's a sight to behold. Because of his normally golden skin tone, Tivernius actually turned a little orange before he spoke.

"After your departure, we interrogated the surviving members of Darkoni's retinue. They told us of his arrangement supplying trolls to the traitor Leothandron, and my queen conjured a portal by which we could observe Leothandron's activities."

"So you guys were sitting there in Faerieland watching the whole thing while we were getting our asses kicked?" I was a little pissed with that mental image.

"Oh, quit your whining and have another beer," Sabrina said. "At least he showed up in time to save your ass."

"I'll drink to that." I clinked my beer bottle to Tivernius' glass.

And I did just that. We sat, and drank, and sat and drank, until finally we had polished off the bottle of scotch as well as a twelve-pack of Miller Lite. When he finished the last of his drink, Tivernius stood, a little unsteadily, and waved a cheery farewell to all of us. He walked to the center of the room, waved his arms, and after a couple of unsuccessful attempts, conjured a portal in the air to take him home.

"I have enjoyed your company this night, and am proud to have fought alongside you. Be well, my friends." And with a wave and a smile, he stepped through the hole in the air, and vanished.

"I will never get used to seeing somebody do that," Sabrina said.

"You probably won't need to, babe. I'm kinda hoping there's not much need for portals to Faerieland in my living room," I said.

"Babe?" she asked, that one eyebrow shooting north.

I tried to return the eyebrow, but without having my face pulverized I could only move them two at a time.

She looked at me trying and laughed. "Call me whatever you want, Jimmy, but for tonight, call me a cab. I'm done."

"Take my bed. The sheets are clean," I said.

"No, I couldn't. I'll cab it home," Sabrina protested.

"Then have to cab it all the way back here tomorrow for your car? That's silly. Go to bed. I'll be fine on the couch. I don't really sleep anyway, remember?"

She started to argue more, then caught sight of Alex and Stephen watching us with smiles on their faces.

"What?" she asked dangerously.

"Nothing, cousin dear. We just think it's cute," Stephen said.

"Think what's cute?" Sabrina asked, voice dripping with danger.

I pretended to be busy getting a blanket out of the linen closet because I didn't need to be around if she shot them. Greg took that opportunity to mutter a quiet "good night" to everyone and run into his room, slamming the door behind him. I guess he'd seen enough bloodshed and brutality for one night.

"You two have never even kissed, and you're acting like an old married couple." Alex laughed while he said it, which might be the only thing that kept him from certain death.

He crossed to Sabrina and gave her a big hug. In the face of his hug and big grin she couldn't even pretend to stay mad. "Cousin, it was wonderful to finally meet you. Now I'm going to take my husband home and put him to bed. Good night everyone, and thank you."

"Yeah, guys. We can't thank you enough," Stephen agreed.

"That's okay, Lenny thanked us plenty," I said, pointing at the cash on the table.

We all laughed again, and the guys headed toward the stairs and into the dawning light. Mike went with them, counting on his clergy bumper sticker to get him out of a Breathalyzer test. Besides, his church was close.

Sabrina and Stephen took a moment at the bottom of the stairs, heads close together, talking softly. When they finished, he headed upstairs with Alex, and she walked back toward me, wiping at her eyes.

"Wanna talk about it?" I asked, holding out a bottle of beer.

"Not really. Family stuff. I thought you were out of beer?"

"We were out of guest beer. We were not out of my private stash." I smiled as I carried my blanket over to the couch.

Sabrina stood at the doorway into my bedroom and looked over at me, holding up her bottle. "I get to drink from the private stash?"

She raised that eyebrow at me again, and I knew it was going to take me a long time to get to sleep.

"Detective, you can drink from whatever you want," I said with a grin.

"Maybe if you play your cards right, I'll tell you the same thing someday," Sabrina said, grinning right back at me.

She turned, walked into my bedroom and closed the door.

About the Author

John G. Hartness is a recovering theatre geek who likes loud music, fried pickles and cold beer. He's also an award-winning poet, lighting designer and theatre producer whose work has been translated into over twenty-five languages and read worldwide. John lives in North Carolina with his lovely wife Suzy and writes full-time.